RSC School Shakespeare

Series consultant: Emma Smith
Professor of Shakespeare Studies
Hertford College, University of Oxford

THE MERCHANT OF VENICE

OXFORD
UNIVERSITY PRESS

OXFORD
UNIVERSITY PRESS

Great Clarendon Street, Oxford, OX2 6DP,
United Kingdom

Oxford University Press is a department of the University of Oxford.
It furthers the University's objective of excellence in research, scholarship,
and education by publishing worldwide. Oxford is a registered trade mark of Oxford
University Press in the UK and in certain other countries

British Library Cataloguing in Publication Data

Data available

ISBN 978-019-836595-2

10 9 8 7 6 5 4 3 2 1

Printed in Great Britain by Bell and Bain Ltd., Glasgow

Acknowledgements

We are indebted to all of those teachers and practitioners who have contributed to
the development of the work in this series. In particular Cicely Berry whose work is a
constant source of inspiration. The material in these editions was primarily written by
RSC Education Associate Practitioners Tracy Irish and Rachel Gartside but we also wish to
acknowledge the contributions of Mary Johnson and Miles Tandy. Editorial work for the
RSC was undertaken by Jacqui O'Hanlon.

Cover and performance images © Royal Shakespeare Company 2018

Cover image by Hugo Glendinning. Other *The Merchant of Venice* performance images by
Hugo Glendinning (2008, 2015) and Ellie Kurttz (2011).

p208(t): © Corbis/Getty Images; p208(m): mashakotcur/Shutterstock; p208(b): Janet Faye
Hastings/Shutterstock; p209(t): 19th era/Alamy Stock Photo; p209(mt): Granger Histori-
cal Picture Archive/Alamy Stock Photo; p209(mb): © National Portrait Gallery, London;
p209(b): Royal Shakespeare Company Theatre Collection; p212: DEA PICTURE LIBRARY/
Getty Images; p214: Gimas/Shutterstock; p215, 216, 219: Royal Shakespeare Company
Theatre Collection.

Layout by Justin Hoffmann at Pixelfox

Contents

Introduction to RSC School Shakespeare

The RSC approach

The classroom as rehearsal room

All the work of RSC Education is underpinned by the artistic practice of the Royal Shakespeare Company (RSC). In particular, we make very strong connections between the rehearsal rooms in which our actors and directors work and the classrooms in which you learn. Rehearsal rooms are essentially places of exploration and shared discovery, in which a company of actors and their director work together to bring Shakespeare's plays to life. To do this successfully they need to have a deep understanding of the text, to get the language 'in the body' and to be open to a range of interpretive possibilities and choices. The ways in which they do this are both active and playful, connecting mind, voice and body.

Becoming a company

To do this we begin by deliberately building a spirit of one group with a shared purpose – this is about 'us' rather than 'me'. We often do this with games that warm up our brains, voices and bodies, and we continue to build this spirit through a scheme of work that includes shared, collaborative tasks that depend on and value everyone's contributions. The ways in which the activities work in this edition encourage discussion, speculation and questioning: there is rarely one right answer. This process requires and develops critical thinking.

Making the world of the play

In rehearsals at the RSC, we explore the whole world of the play: we tackle the language, characters and motivation, setting, plot and themes. By 'standing in the shoes' of the characters and exploring the world of the play, you will be engaged fully: head, eyes, ears, hands, bodies and hearts are involved in actively interpreting the play. In grappling with scenes and speeches, you are also actively grappling with the themes and ideas in the play, experiencing them from the points of view of the different characters.

RSC rehearsal

The language is central to our discoveries

We place the language in the plays at the core of everything we do. Active, playful approaches can make Shakespeare's words vivid, accessible and enjoyable. His language has the power to excite and delight all of us.

In the rehearsal room, the RSC uses social and historical context in order to deepen understanding of the world of the play. The company is engaged in a 'conversation across time', inviting audiences to consider what a play means to us now and what it meant to us then. We hope that the activities in this edition will offer you an opportunity to join that conversation.

The activities require close, critical reading and encourage you to make informed interpretive choices about language, character and motivation, themes and plot. The work is rooted in speaking and listening to Shakespeare's words and to each other's ideas in order to help embrace and unlock this extraordinary literary inheritance.

Jacqui O'Hanlon
Director of Education
Royal Shakespeare Company

The Royal Shakespeare Theatre

Using *RSC School Shakespeare*

As you open each double page, you will see the script of the play on the right-hand page. On the left-hand page is a series of features that will help you connect with and explore William Shakespeare's play *The Merchant of Venice* and the world in which Shakespeare lived.

Those features are:

Summary

At the top of every left-hand page is a summary of what happens on the facing page to help you understand the action.

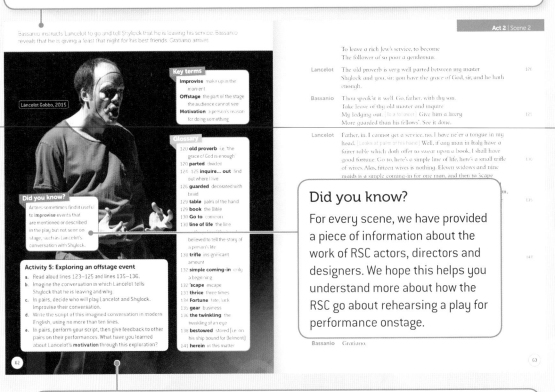

RSC performance photographs

Every left-hand page includes at least one photograph from an RSC production of the play. Some of the activities make direct use of the production photographs. The photographs illustrate the action, bringing to life the text on the facing page. They also include a caption that identifies the character or event, together with the date of the RSC production.

Did you know?

For every scene, we have provided a piece of information about the work of RSC actors, directors and designers. We hope this helps you understand more about how the RSC go about rehearsing a play for performance onstage.

At the time

There are social and historical research tasks, so that you can use knowledge from the time the play was written to help you interpret the text of the play. The social and historical information can be found on pages 208–222 of this edition.

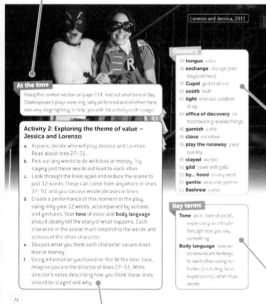

Jessica, disguised in a boy's costume, comes to her window. She throws down a casket of money and jewels. Lorenzo urges her to come down so that they can run away to Bassanio's feast. Jessica says she will be straight down after she has locked up and collected some more money.

[Lorenzo and Jessica, 2011]

Enter Jessica above in boy's clothes

Jessica	Who are you? Tell me, for more certainty, Albeit I'll swear that I do know your tongue.
Lorenzo	Lorenzo, and thy love.
Jessica	Lorenzo, certain, and my love indeed, For who love I so much? And now who knows But you, Lorenzo, whether I am yours?
Lorenzo	Heaven and thy thoughts are witness that thou art.
Jessica	Here, catch this casket, it is worth the pains. I am glad 'tis night, you do not look on me, For I am much ashamed of my exchange. But love is blind and lovers cannot see The pretty follies that themselves commit, For if they could, Cupid himself would blush To see me thus transformèd to a boy.

Glossary

28 **tongue** voice

31 **exchange** change (into boy's clothes)

39 **Cupid** god of desire

43 **sooth** truth

43 **light** immoral, evident, lit up

44 **office of discovery** i.e. torchbearing reveals things

46 **garnish** outfit

48 **close** secretive

48 **play the runaway** pass quickly

49 **stayed** waited

50 **gild** cover with gold

52 **by... hood** on my word

52 **gentle** dear one, gentle

53 **Beshrew** curse

Glossary

Where needed, there is a glossary that explains words from the play that may be unfamiliar and cannot be worked out in context.

At the time

Using the context section on page 214, find out what time of day Shakespeare's plays were originally performed and whether there was any stage lighting, to help you with the activity on this page.

Activity 2: Exploring the theme of value – Jessica and Lorenzo

a. In pairs, decide who will play Jessica and Lorenzo. Read aloud lines 27–51.

b. Pick out any words to do with love or money. Try saying just these words out loud to each other.

c. Look through the lines again and reduce the scene to just 12 words. These can come from anywhere in lines 27–51 and you can use whole phrases or lines.

d. Create a performance of this moment in the play, using only your 12 words, accompanied by actions and gestures. Your **tone** of voice and **body language** should clearly tell the story of what happens. Each character in the scene must respond to the words and actions of the other character.

e. Discuss what you think each character values most: love or money.

f. Using information you found for the 'At the time' task, imagine you are the director of lines 27–51. Write director's notes describing how you think these lines should be staged and why.

Key terms

Tone as in 'tone of voice', expressing an attitude through how you say something

Body language how we communicate feelings to each other using our bodies (including facial expressions) rather than words

Key terms

Where needed, there is an explanation of any key terms used, literary or theatrical.

Exit Jessica above

Gratiano	Now, by my hood, a gentle and no Jew.
Lorenzo	Beshrew me but I love her heartily For she is wise, if I can judge of her, And fair she is, if that mine eyes be true,

Activity

Every left-hand page includes at least one activity that is inspired by RSC rehearsal room practice.

Introducing *The Merchant of Venice*

The play in performance

The Merchant of Venice was written between 1596 and 1598. It was first performed at the court of King James I in 1605. At the Royal Shakespeare Company (RSC), we have staged the play many times and each interpretation is completely different. Shakespeare's plays are packed full of questions and challenges for the director, designer and acting company to solve. The clues to finding the answers are always somewhere in the text, but the possibilities for interpretation are infinite.

Portia and Nerissa, 2011

A place of possibilities

The Merchant of Venice is a really exciting play to work on, but it also presents some real challenges for the director and actors tasked with bringing it to life on stage.

For any director starting to work on bringing *The Merchant of Venice* to life for a contemporary audience, there are lots of interpretive choices to be made.

Jessica and Lorenzo, 2008

From creating the worlds of Belmont and Venice, to defining the kind of relationship that exists between Antonio and Bassanio; the play is full of challenges and choices. Over the course of a six to eight-week rehearsal period, actors and their director will try out different options, they will explore different ways of playing scenes informed always by the clues that Shakespeare gives them; they effectively become text detectives, mining the language for clues to help inform their performance choices.

We have taken all of the ways of working of our actors and directors and set them alongside the text of *The Merchant of Venice* which, together with the other titles in the series, offers a great introduction to Shakespeare's world and work. An actor once described the rehearsal room to me as a 'place of possibilities'. I think that's a wonderful way of thinking about a classroom too and it's what we hope the RSC School Shakespeare editions help to create.

Jacqui O'Hanlon
Director of Education
Royal Shakespeare Company

The play at a glance

Every scene in a play presents a challenge to the actors and their director in terms of how to stage it. There are certain key moments in a play that directors need to pay special attention to because they contain really significant events.

The scene is set (Act 1 Scene 1)

Antonio's friend Bassanio visits him and asks to borrow a large sum of money. He has borrowed from Antonio before and lost it all. But this time he needs it in his attempt to win and marry Portia. Antonio feels for Bassanio – he would lend him the money if he had it but all his capital is tied up with the return of his ships. Antonio suggests that his credit might be good for a loan in town.

Portia (Act 1 Scene 2)

Portia is an heiress and lives outside of Venice itself in Belmont. She is rich, beautiful and brilliant. Bassanio is in love with her and he thinks she is interested in him. There is a challenge for any man who wants to claim Portia. He must choose between three caskets. One is gold, one silver and the last is lead.

Portia and Nerissa, 2015

Pound of flesh (Act 1 Scene 3)

Bassanio tries to secure a loan from Shylock, who is a money-lender and a Jew. Shylock has suffered insults from Antonio in the past but Shylock does agree to a loan of three thousand ducats. If his money is not returned within three months then Shylock will reclaim his bond in the form of a pound of Antonio's flesh. Bassanio is chilled by this violent request but Antonio assures him that the money will be safely returned to Shylock as his ships are all soon coming in.

Jessica's plan (Act 2 Scene 3)

Shylock's daughter, Jessica, reveals to the audience that she plans to convert to Christianity and marry her Christian lover, Lorenzo.

Bassanio chooses a casket (Act 3 Scene 2)

All of Portia's suitors have chosen the wrong casket and she is very relieved. Bassanio arrives to view the caskets and read their riddles. He decides on the leaden casket and, in doing so, he wins her. Bassanio marries Portia while his friend Gratiano weds her maid, Nerissa, who he has been wooing.

Portia and the Prince of Arragon, 2011

Shylock, 2011

Bad news (Act 3 Scene 2)

Antonio is certain his ships have in fact floundered at sea and he has been arrested on account of his debt to Shylock. Portia sweeps away Bassanio's fears saying she will pay back six thousand ducats to Shylock. But Shylock refuses this offer of doubled repayment. The only settlement he will accept is his pound of flesh which the lawful contract has promised him.

The court (Act 4 Scene 1)

A court is held to confirm whether Shylock can take his pound of flesh from Antonio. Portia and Nerissa dress up as a young lawyer and a clerk working for Antonio. Bassanio and Gratiano watch the proceedings but do not recognise their wives. Portia conducts a brilliant defence and tries to change Shylock's mind.

But Shylock is adamant and the court has to agree that the law is on his side; he prepares his knife. Portia declares that he is indeed entitled to a pound of flesh. But if Shylock sheds blood or the bloodless flesh weighs an ounce outside an exact pound then he will be tried for murder. She also says that Shylock should forfeit his life for having conspired against the life of a Venetian.

The court rules against Shylock and orders him to give half of his money to Antonio and the other half to the State. Antonio protests that Shylock can keep his half but that Shylock must now convert to Christianity and leave his property to Jessica whom he disinherited for running away with Lorenzo. Shylock agrees, beaten, sick with the disgrace and humiliation.

Bassanio and Gratiano are so impressed by the 'lawyer' and his 'clerk' that they gave them their wedding rings.

Good news (Act 5 Scene 1)

Portia and Nerissa return out of disguise and ask Bassanio and Gratiano where their rings are. The men are panicked but the women finally confess to having been disguised. There is fresh news about Antonio's ships: they have been saved.

Portia, Antonio, Bassanio and Gratiano, 2015

The Merchant of Venice

Antonio, a merchant of Venice
Bassanio, friend of Antonio, suitor to Portia
Lorenzo, friend of Antonio and Bassanio, elopes with Jessica
Gratiano, friend of Antonio and Bassanio, suitor to Nerissa
Salarino, friend of Antonio
Solanio, friend of Antonio
Leonardo, Servant to Bassanio
Portia, an heiress
Nerissa, Portia's gentlewoman-in-waiting
Balthasar, Servant to Portia
Stephano, Servant to Portia
Prince of Arragon, suitor to Portia
Prince of Morocco, suitor to Portia

Shylock, a Jew of Venice
Jessica, Shylock's daughter
Tubal, Shylock's friend
Lancelot Gobbo, the clown, Servant to Shylock and later to Bassanio
Old Gobbo, Lancelot's father

Duke of Venice
Magnificoes of Venice
Salerio, a messenger from Venice
A Jailer, Attendants and Servants

Antonio, a merchant of Venice, is depressed. His friends Salarino and Solanio think that he is worried about his ships at sea.

Antonio (far right), 2011

At the time

Using the context section on page 213, find out what Shakespeare's audience thought of Venice, to help you with the activity on this page.

Activity 1: Exploring performance through design

a. Look at the photo on this page, which shows Venice brought to life as a modern casino.
b. Write designer's notes on what you can see. Be as detailed as you can, describing the colours and textures, as well as the things in the photo.
c. Using what you have found out about Venice on page 213, discuss:
   i. why you think the designer of this production chose to set the play in a modern casino
   ii. how effective you think this idea is.
d. Summarise your analysis of the designer's choices in a paragraph.

Glossary

s.d. **Salarino** Some editors call this character 'Salerio', doubling Antonio's friend with Portia's messenger

1 **sooth** truth

6 **want-wit** fool

7 **ado** trouble

9 **argosies** large merchant ships

9 **portly** dignified

10 **signors** gentlemen

10 **burghers** townspeople

10 **flood** sea

11 **pageants** carnival floats

12 **overpeer** look over

12 **petty traffickers** small trading boats

14 **woven wings** sails

15 **venture forth** business abroad

18 **Plucking… wind** using a blade of grass to see which way the wind blows

19 **roads** safe places to anchor

22 **wind** breath

23 **ague** fever

27 **my wealthy Andrew** my own richly laden ship

28 **Vailing… ribs** lowering her main mast below her wooden sides

Act 1 | Scene 1

Enter Antonio, Salarino and Solanio

Antonio   In sooth I know not why I am so sad.
It wearies me, you say it wearies you;
But how I caught it, found it, or came by it,
What stuff 'tis made of, whereof it is born,
I am to learn;   5
And such a want-wit sadness makes of me,
That I have much ado to know myself.

Salarino   Your mind is tossing on the ocean,
There where your argosies with portly sail
Like signors and rich burghers on the flood,   10
Or as it were the pageants of the sea,
Do overpeer the petty traffickers
That curtsy to them, do them reverence,
As they fly by them with their woven wings.

Solanio   Believe me, sir, had I such venture forth,   15
The better part of my affections would
Be with my hopes abroad. I should be still
Plucking the grass to know where sits the wind,
Peering in maps for ports and piers and roads,
And every object that might make me fear   20
Misfortune to my ventures, out of doubt
Would make me sad.

Salarino   My wind cooling my broth
Would blow me to an ague when I thought
What harm a wind too great might do at sea.
I should not see the sandy hour-glass run,   25
But I should think of shallows and of flats,
And see my wealthy Andrew docked in sand,
Vailing her high top lower than her ribs

Antonio denies that he is worried about his merchandise at sea, so his friends ask him if he is depressed because he is in love. They try to cheer him up. Bassanio, Lorenzo and Gratiano arrive.

Glossary

33 **stream** current
34 **silks** Silk was an expensive cargo
35 **even... this** in this moment worth a fortune
42 **bottom** ship
46 **Fie, fie** expression of disapproval
50 **Janus** Roman god of openings, who faced both directions at once
54 **vinegar aspect** sour-faced
56 **Nestor** wise, trusted Greek general

Solanio, Salarino and Antonio, 2011

Key terms

Director the person who enables the practical and creative interpretation of a dramatic script, and ultimately brings together everybody's ideas in a way that engages the audience with the play

Themes the main ideas explored in a piece of literature, e.g. the themes of love and friendship, fathers and daughters, justice and mercy, prejudice, deceptive appearances and value might be considered key themes of *The Merchant of Venice*

Adjective a word that describes a noun, e.g. *blue*, *happy*, *big*

Activity 2: Exploring the themes of love and friendship – Antonio

a. In groups, decide who will play Antonio, Salarino and Solanio.
b. Read aloud lines 39–50 twice:
   i. as if Salarino and Solanio know that being in love is definitely the cause of Antonio's depression
   ii. as if Salarino and Solanio genuinely do not know why Antonio is depressed.
c. Discuss which version felt most appropriate for each character and why.
d. Write a list of **adjectives** you would use to describe Antonio in lines 1–50.

To kiss her burial. Should I go to church
And see the holy edifice of stone,   30
And not bethink me straight of dangerous rocks,
Which touching but my gentle vessel's side,
Would scatter all her spices on the stream,
Enrobe the roaring waters with my silks,
And in a word, but even now worth this,   35
And now worth nothing? Shall I have the thought
To think on this, and shall I lack the thought
That such a thing bechanced would make me sad?
But tell not me, I know Antonio
Is sad to think upon his merchandise.   40

Antonio   Believe me, no. I thank my fortune for it,
My ventures are not in one bottom trusted,
Nor to one place; nor is my whole estate
Upon the fortune of this present year.
Therefore my merchandise makes me not sad.   45

Solanio   Why then you are in love.

Antonio   Fie, fie.

Solanio   Not in love neither. Then let us say you are sad
Because you are not merry; and 'twere as easy
For you to laugh and leap, and say you are merry
Because you are not sad. Now, by two-headed Janus,   50
Nature hath framed strange fellows in her time:
Some that will evermore peep through their eyes
And laugh like parrots at a bagpiper,
And other of such vinegar aspect
That they'll not show their teeth in way of smile,   55
Though Nestor swear the jest be laughable.

Enter Bassanio, Lorenzo and Gratiano

Here comes Bassanio your most noble kinsman,
Gratiano, and Lorenzo. Fare ye well,
We leave you now with better company.

Salarino   I would have stayed till I had made you merry,   60

Salarino and Solanio leave Antonio with Bassanio, Lorenzo and Gratiano. Gratiano tries to cheer Antonio up.

Did you know?

Shakespeare's plays were first performed in theatres where the audience surrounded three sides of the stage. This meant that even when there were other characters visible at the back of the stage, two or three characters could come forwards to have a private moment between themselves, and the audience could see and hear that moment clearly. In rehearsals, actors have to work out the extent to which the other characters on stage are aware of those moments. That is, how private or public they are.

Activity 3: Exploring how private or public a moment is

a. In pairs, decide who will play Gratiano and Antonio. Read aloud lines 73–90.

b. Read the lines again, but this time whisper them as if Gratiano and Antonio do not want to be overheard by the other characters. How does this change the moment?

c. Stand five paces apart and read the lines again, this time loudly, as if neither character cares who overhears them.

d. Read the lines again, this time varying the volume of your speech according to how you think lines 73–90 should be played.

e. Discuss what you think the other characters should be doing during lines 73–90.

f. If you were going to stage this moment, how private or public would you make it? Give reasons for your answer.

Glossary

67 **strange** distant

68 **We'll… yours** we'll make ourselves free when you are

74 **upon** for

75 **They… care** those that care too much about the world lose the ability to live in it

84 **his… alabaster** a statue of his grandfather

85 **jaundice** disease of the liver

88 **visages** faces

89 **cream and mantle** stagnate and become overgrown

90 **wilful stillness** stubborn silence

	If worthier friends had not prevented me.	
Antonio	Your worth is very dear in my regard.	
	I take it your own business calls on you,	
	And you embrace th'occasion to depart.	
Salarino	Good morrow, my good lords.	65
Bassanio	Good signors both, when shall we laugh? Say, when?	
	You grow exceeding strange. Must it be so?	
Salarino	We'll make our leisures to attend on yours.	

Exeunt Salarino and Solanio

Lorenzo	My Lord Bassanio, since you have found Antonio,	
	We two will leave you, but at dinnertime	70
	I pray you have in mind where we must meet.	
Bassanio	I will not fail you.	
Gratiano	You look not well, Signor Antonio,	
	You have too much respect upon the world.	
	They lose it that do buy it with much care.	75
	Believe me, you are marvellously changed.	
Antonio	I hold the world but as the world, Gratiano,	
	A stage where every man must play a part,	
	And mine a sad one.	
Gratiano	Let me play the fool;	
	With mirth and laughter let old wrinkles come,	80
	And let my liver rather heat with wine	
	Than my heart cool with mortifying groans.	
	Why should a man whose blood is warm within,	
	Sit like his grandsire, cut in alabaster?	
	Sleep when he wakes? And creep into the jaundice	85
	By being peevish? I tell thee what, Antonio,	
	I love thee, and it is my love that speaks:	
	There are a sort of men whose visages	
	Do cream and mantle like a standing pond,	
	And do a wilful stillness entertain,	90

Gratiano advises Antonio not to get a reputation for being melancholy, before leaving with Lorenzo. When everyone else has gone, Antonio asks Bassanio about his secret plans to visit a woman.

Antonio and Gratiano, 2015

Glossary

91 **dressed... opinion** get a reputation
92 **conceit** thought
93 **oracle** holder of divine truth
94 **ope** open
94 **let... bark** let nothing interrupt
102 **gudgeon** easily caught fish
104 **exhortation** sermon
110 **grow... gear** talk more for this reason
112 **neat's tongue** ox tongue
112 **vendible** marriageable
116 **ere** before

Activity 4: Exploring a character — Gratiano

a. In groups, decide who will play Lorenzo, Gratiano, Antonio and Bassanio. Read aloud lines 103–112.
b. Write down the two phrases that the other characters say about Gratiano in lines 103–112.
c. **Paraphrase** each of the phrases from task b.
d. Work together to help the person playing Gratiano make a **statue** of Gratiano as the other characters see him.
e. The people playing the other characters choose a phrase from task b. Read your chosen phrases, whilst Gratiano brings the statue you have created to life.
f. Share your work with another group, explaining the choices you made.
g. Write a paragraph that explains the attitudes of Gratiano's friends towards him, using quotations from lines 103–112.

Key terms

Paraphrase put a line or section of text into your own words
Statue like a **freeze-frame** but usually of a single character
Freeze-frame a physical, still image created by people to represent an object, place, person or feeling

With purpose to be dressed in an opinion
Of wisdom, gravity, profound conceit,
As who should say, 'I am, sir, an oracle,
And when I ope my lips, let no dog bark.'
O my Antonio, I do know of these   95
That therefore only are reputed wise
For saying nothing, when I am very sure
If they should speak, would almost damn those ears
Which, hearing them, would call their brothers fools.
I'll tell thee more of this another time.   100
But fish not with this melancholy bait
For this fool gudgeon, this opinion.
Come, good Lorenzo. Fare ye well awhile,
I'll end my exhortation after dinner.

Lorenzo   Well, we will leave you then till dinnertime.   105
I must be one of these same dumb wise men,
For Gratiano never lets me speak.

Gratiano   Well, keep me company but two years more,
Thou shalt not know the sound of thine own tongue.

Antonio   Fare you well, I'll grow a talker for this gear.   110

Gratiano   Thanks, i'faith, for silence is only commendable
In a neat's tongue dried and a maid not vendible.

Exeunt Gratiano and Lorenzo

Antonio   Is that anything now?

Bassanio   Gratiano speaks an infinite deal of nothing, more than any man
in all Venice. His reasons are as two grains of wheat hid in two   115
bushels of chaff. You shall seek all day ere you find them, and
when you have them, they are not worth the search.

Antonio   Well, tell me now, what lady is the same
To whom you swore a secret pilgrimage
That you today promised to tell me of?   120

Bassanio   'Tis not unknown to you, Antonio,
How much I have disabled mine estate

Bassanio reminds Antonio that he is in debt. Antonio offers to help Bassanio in any way that he can, as he has done before.

Antonio and Bassanio, 2008

At the time

Using the context section on page 221, find out how Shakespeare's audience would have understood male friendship, to help you with the activity on this page.

Key terms

Motivation a person's reason for doing something
Back-story what happened to any of the characters before the start of the play

Activity 5: Exploring back-story and the themes of love and friendship

In pairs, decide who will play Antonio and Bassanio. Read aloud lines 134–159.

a. Discuss what Antonio's **motivation** might be for lending Bassanio money.
b. Using information you found for the 'At the time' task and the clues in lines 134–159, discuss what the **back-story** of their relationship might be. Consider how they met, the reasons why Antonio might have lent money to Bassanio previously and the ways in which Bassanio might have lost that money. You may have several ideas.
c. Choose one of your ideas and create three freeze-frames that tell the beginning, middle and end of Antonio and Bassanio's back-story.
d. Write the back-story from Antonio's point of view, using the ideas of love and friendship.

Glossary

123 **swelling port** richer lifestyle
124 **faint means** weak spending power
126 **rate** way of living
127 **come fairly off** get myself out honourably
128 **prodigal** Bassanio seems to compare himself to the prodigal son in the Bible (Luke 15), who spent his inheritance on luxury living
129 **gaged** owing
138 **occasions** needs
139 **shaft** arrow
140 **his... flight** another arrow exactly the same weight
141 **advisèd** careful
142 **adventuring** risking
151 **rest debtor** remain in your debt
152 **herein... time** now only waste time
153 **circumstance** your situation
155 **making... uttermost** questioning that I will do everything I can for you

By something showing a more swelling port
Than my faint means would grant continuance.
Nor do I now make moan to be abridged   125
From such a noble rate, but my chief care
Is to come fairly off from the great debts
Wherein my time something too prodigal
Hath left me gaged. To you, Antonio,
I owe the most in money and in love,   130
And from your love I have a warranty
To unburden all my plots and purposes
How to get clear of all the debts I owe.

Antonio   I pray you, good Bassanio, let me know it,
And if it stand as you yourself still do,   135
Within the eye of honour, be assured
My purse, my person, my extremest means,
Lie all unlocked to your occasions.

Bassanio   In my schooldays, when I had lost one shaft,
I shot his fellow of the selfsame flight   140
The selfsame way with more advisèd watch
To find the other forth, and by adventuring both
I oft found both. I urge this childhood proof
Because what follows is pure innocence.
I owe you much, and like a wilful youth,   145
That which I owe is lost. But if you please
To shoot another arrow that self way
Which you did shoot the first, I do not doubt,
As I will watch the aim, or to find both,
Or bring your latter hazard back again,   150
And thankfully rest debtor for the first.

Antonio   You know me well, and herein spend but time
To wind about my love with circumstance,
And out of doubt you do me now more wrong
In making question of my uttermost   155
Than if you had made waste of all I have.
Then do but say to me what I should do
That in your knowledge may by me be done,

Bassanio explains he needs to borrow money to woo Portia. Antonio's money is all invested in merchant ships at sea, so he offers to take out a loan. They go to find a moneylender.

Bassanio and Antonio, 2015

Activity 6: Exploring the themes of love and friendship – Antonio and Bassanio

a. Look back through Act 1 Scene 1 to remind yourself of what happens.

b. Discuss the following questions, thinking about both Antonio and Bassanio:

   i. How does the character feel when he first enters the scene? Is there any change in this emotion by the time he leaves?

   ii. How do Antonio and Bassanio react to one another during this scene?

   iii. How might this affect each of their states of mind and their feelings towards one another?

c. Look at the photo on this page. Which moment in Act 1 Scene 1 would you say this was, and why?

d. Write a character profile for Antonio or Bassanio based on what you discovered in Act 1 Scene 1. Include ideas about love and friendship, and use relevant quotations.

Glossary

159 **pressed unto** ready for

160 **richly left** inherited a fortune

164–165 **nothing... Portia** as worthy as the Roman Portia, wife of Brutus

169 **golden fleece** in Greek mythology, one of the treasures searched for by Jason

170 **seat** house

170 **Colchos' strand** the shore on which the golden fleece was found

174 **presages** that predicts

174 **thrift** profit

179 **Try... do** see if anyone in Venice will lend me money

180 **racked** stretched

181 **furnish thee** equip you to go

184 **of my trust** on my credit

And I am pressed unto it. Therefore speak.

Bassanio   In Belmont is a lady richly left,   160
And she is fair and, fairer than that word,
Of wondrous virtues. Sometimes from her eyes
I did receive fair speechless messages.
Her name is Portia, nothing undervalued
To Cato's daughter, Brutus' Portia.   165
Nor is the wide world ignorant of her worth,
For the four winds blow in from every coast
Renownèd suitors, and her sunny locks
Hang on her temples like a golden fleece,
Which makes her seat of Belmont Colchos' strand,   170
And many Jasons come in quest of her.
O my Antonio, had I but the means
To hold a rival place with one of them,
I have a mind presages me such thrift,
That I should questionless be fortunate.   175

Antonio   Thou know'st that all my fortunes are at sea,
Neither have I money, nor commodity
To raise a present sum; therefore go forth,
Try what my credit can in Venice do,
That shall be racked, even to the uttermost,   180
To furnish thee to Belmont, to fair Portia.
Go presently inquire, and so will I,
Where money is, and I no question make
To have it of my trust or for my sake.

Exeunt

In Belmont, Portia explains to her companion Nerissa that, because of her dead father's will, Portia's suitors have to choose between caskets of gold, silver and lead. Whoever chooses the one her father intended can marry her.

Portia and Nerissa, 2015

At the time

Using the context section on page 217, find out what Shakespeare's main sources for *The Merchant of Venice* were, to help you with the activity on this page.

Activity 1: Exploring the theme of fathers and daughters

a. In pairs, decide who will play Portia and Nerissa. Read aloud lines 18–26.

b. Create a freeze-frame of the characters at this moment in the play.

c. Still in your freeze-frame, take turns to speak aloud your thoughts from the point of view of your character.

d. What have you learned about Portia and Nerissa from tasks a–c?

e. Using information you found for the 'At the time' task, discuss:
   i. the ways that Shakespeare changed the story of the caskets for his play
   ii. the effects of these changes.

f. Write a paragraph that explains why you think Shakespeare changed the story of the caskets for his play, including ideas about fathers and daughters in your response.

Glossary

s.d. **waiting woman** confidante and companion

1 **troth** faith

3 **aught** anything

6 **mean** middle

6 **Superfluity** overindulgence

6 **competency** sufficiency

8 **sentences** proverbs

12 **divine** clergyman

15 **blood** passion

15 **cold decree** reasonable advice

15–17 **such… cripple** young love easily escapes the crippling trap of sensible advice

18 **would** prefer

19 **will** desire

20 **will** last will and testament

25 **his meaning** the one your father intended

Act 1 | Scene 2

Enter Portia with her waiting woman Nerissa

Portia   By my troth, Nerissa, my little body is aweary of this great world.

Nerissa   You would be, sweet madam, if your miseries were in the same abundance as your good fortunes are, and yet, for aught I see, they are as sick that surfeit with too much as they that starve with nothing. It is no small happiness, therefore, to be seated in the   5 mean. Superfluity comes sooner by white hairs, but competency lives longer.

Portia   Good sentences and well pronounced.

Nerissa   They would be better if well followed.

Portia   If to do were as easy as to know what were good to do, chapels   10 had been churches and poor men's cottages princes' palaces. It is a good divine that follows his own instructions. I can easier teach twenty what were good to be done than be one of the twenty to follow mine own teaching. The brain may devise laws for the blood, but a hot temper leaps o'er a cold decree; such a hare is   15 madness the youth, to skip o'er the meshes of good counsel the cripple. But this reason is not in fashion to choose me a husband. O me, the word 'choose'. I may neither choose whom I would, nor refuse whom I dislike, so is the will of a living daughter curbed by the will of a dead father. Is it not hard, Nerissa, that I cannot   20 choose one nor refuse none?

Nerissa   Your father was ever virtuous, and holy men at their death have good inspirations. Therefore the lottery that he hath devised in these three chests of gold, silver and lead, whereof who chooses his meaning chooses you, will no doubt never be chosen by any   25 rightly but one who you shall rightly love. But what warmth is there in your affection towards any of these princely suitors that are already come?

Did you know?

The director and actors at the RSC typically spend six weeks in full-time rehearsals for a play like *The Merchant of Venice*. They spend time reading through the play and putting it into their own words, so that they have agreed what the words mean to them. Then, they get up on their feet to explore Shakespeare's original text.

Nerissa and Portia, 2011

Glossary

29 **overname** list
30 **level** guess
32 **Neapolitan** People from Naples were stereotypically good with horses
33 **colt** foolish young man; young horse
34 **appropriation** addition
34 **parts** abilities
36 **smith** blacksmith
37 **County Palatine** count with royal privileges
38 **as... say** as if to say
40 **weeping philosopher** Heraclitus of Ephesus, who gave up his throne and became a recluse
42 **death's-head** skull
47 **better bad** worse
48 **He... man** He copies everyone else but has no identity of his own
48 **throstle** thrush
49 **a capering** to dancing
57 **proper man's picture** handsome
59 **doublet** sleeveless tunic
59 **round hose** padded trousers

Activity 2: Exploring Portia's suitors and the theme of deceptive appearances

a. In pairs, decide who will play Portia and Nerissa. Read aloud lines 29–60.
b. Choose one of the suitors that Portia talks about.
c. Paraphrase what Portia says about the suitor you have chosen.
d. Work together to create a statue of your chosen suitor as Portia sees him. The person playing Nerissa should become the statue of the suitor.
e. The person playing Portia should read what Portia says about the suitor, whilst the person playing Nerissa brings the statue you have created to life.
f. Share your work with another pair. Explain the choices you made, talking about the theme of deceptive appearances.
g. Rewrite lines 29–60 in your own words.

Portia	I pray thee overname them, and as thou namest them, I will describe them, and according to my description level at my affection.
Nerissa	First there is the Neapolitan prince.
Portia	Ay that's a colt indeed, for he doth nothing but talk of his horse, and he makes it a great appropriation to his own good parts that he can shoe him himself. I am much afraid my lady his mother played false with a smith.
Nerissa	Then is there the County Palatine.
Portia	He doth nothing but frown, as who should say, 'And you will not have me, choose.' He hears merry tales and smiles not. I fear he will prove the weeping philosopher when he grows old, being so full of unmannerly sadness in his youth. I had rather to be married to a death's-head with a bone in his mouth than to either of these. God defend me from these two.
Nerissa	How say you by the French lord, Monsieur Le Bon?
Portia	God made him, and therefore let him pass for a man. In truth, I know it is a sin to be a mocker, but he, why he hath a horse better than the Neapolitan's, a better bad habit of frowning than the Count Palatine. He is every man in no man. If a throstle sing, he falls straight a capering. He will fence with his own shadow. If I should marry him, I should marry twenty husbands. If he would despise me, I would forgive him, for if he love me to madness, I should never requite him.
Nerissa	What say you then to Falconbridge, the young baron of England?
Portia	You know I say nothing to him, for he understands not me, nor I him. He hath neither Latin, French, nor Italian, and you will come into the court and swear that I have a poor pennyworth in the English. He is a proper man's picture, but alas, who can converse with a dumb show? How oddly he is suited. I think he bought his doublet in Italy, his round hose in France, his bonnet in Germany, and his behaviour everywhere.
Nerissa	What think you of the Scottish lord, his neighbour?

30

35

40

45

50

55

60

Nerissa reassures her mistress that all the suitors have decided to return to their homes, to Portia's relief. Nerissa reminds Portia that Bassanio visited them when Portia's father was alive. They both remember him well.

Portia and Nerissa, 2008

Activity 3: Exploring the themes of love and friendship – Portia

a. In pairs, decide who will play Portia and Nerissa. Read aloud lines 79–95.

b. Read the lines again, but this time whisper them as if the characters are talking about something secret.

c. Stand about five steps apart and read the lines again, loudly, as if the characters do not care who hears them.

d. Discuss how these different approaches change your understanding of the scene.

e. Finally, read the lines again, this time varying the volume of your speech according to how you think the scene should be performed. Discuss:

   i.   how you think Portia is feeling during lines 79–95

   ii. why you think Nerissa reminds Portia about Bassanio at this moment.

f. Write a paragraph explaining why you think Shakespeare included this moment in the play and how it contributes to the themes of love and friendship.

Glossary

62–63 borrowed... ear got his ears boxed by

64 surety guarantor

65 sealed... another used his wax seal to promise another blow to the ear

70 make shift arrange

76 Rhenish wine fine white wine

78 sponge alcoholic

82 sort way

84 Sibylla in classical mythology, a prophetess who lived for many years

84 Diana Roman goddess of chastity

86 parcel company

90 scholar... soldier This was the perfect man in the Renaissance

91 Montferrat Italian dukedom

93 foolish inexperienced

Portia	That he hath a neighbourly charity in him, for he borrowed a box of the ear of the Englishman and swore he would pay him again when he was able. I think the Frenchman became his surety and sealed under for another.
Nerissa	How like you the young German, the Duke of Saxony's nephew?
Portia	Very vilely in the morning when he is sober, and most vilely in the afternoon when he is drunk. When he is best, he is a little worse than a man, and when he is worst, he is little better than a beast. And the worst fall that ever fell, I hope I shall make shift to go without him.
Nerissa	If he should offer to choose, and choose the right casket, you should refuse to perform your father's will, if you should refuse to accept him.
Portia	Therefore, for fear of the worst, I pray thee set a deep glass of Rhenish wine on the contrary casket, for if the devil be within, and that temptation without, I know he will choose it. I will do anything, Nerissa, ere I will be married to a sponge.
Nerissa	You need not fear, lady, the having any of these lords. They have acquainted me with their determinations, which is indeed to return to their home, and to trouble you with no more suit, unless you may be won by some other sort than your father's imposition, depending on the caskets.
Portia	If I live to be as old as Sibylla, I will die as chaste as Diana, unless I be obtained by the manner of my father's will. I am glad this parcel of wooers are so reasonable, for there is not one among them but I dote on his very absence, and I wish them a fair departure.
Nerissa	Do you not remember, lady, in your father's time, a Venetian, a scholar and a soldier, that came hither in company of the Marquis of Montferrat?
Portia	Yes, yes, it was Bassanio, as I think, so was he called.
Nerissa	True, madam. He of all the men that ever my foolish eyes looked upon, was the best deserving a fair lady.

65

70

75

80

85

90

A servant comes to let Portia know that the suitors are leaving but that the Prince of Morocco will be arriving that night. Portia is not looking forward to his visit.

Activity 4: Exploring Portia

a. Look back through Act 1 Scenes 1–2.
b. Draw an outline of a human figure to represent Portia.
c. Using information you found for the 'At the time' task, around the outside of the figure, write down everything you have found out about Portia so far, including what other characters say about her and what her relationships are. Remember to include her dead father. Write down what you know about the world she lives in. Use your own words and quotations from Act 1 Scenes 1–2.
d. Inside the outline, write down how Portia feels and what her secrets are, in your own words and using quotations from Act 1 Scenes 1–2.
e. Write a character profile for Portia at this point in the play.

At the time

Using the context section on page 222, find out how society expected women to behave, to help you with the activity on this page.

Glossary

97 **four strangers** four foreign suitors (Portia has described six)
102 **condition** appearance
102 **complexion… devil** traditionally, black
103 **shrive** hear my confession
103 **wive** marry
103 **Sirrah** sir (term used to an inferior)

Portia I remember him well, and I remember him worthy of thy praise. 95

Enter a Servingman

How now, what news?

Servant The four strangers seek you, madam, to take their leave. And there
is a forerunner come from a fifth, the Prince of Morocco, who
brings word the Prince his master will be here tonight.

Portia If I could bid the fifth welcome with so good heart as I can bid 100
the other four farewell, I should be glad of his approach. If he
have the condition of a saint and the complexion of a devil, I had
rather he should shrive me than wive me. Come, Nerissa. Sirrah,
go before. Whiles we shut the gate upon one wooer, another
knocks at the door. 105

Exeunt

In Venice, Bassanio asks Shylock the moneylender if he will make a loan of 3000 ducats, for three months, which Antonio will be bound to pay back.

Shylock and Antonio, 2011

Activity 1: Exploring objectives and tactics

a. In pairs, decide who will play Shylock and Bassanio. Read aloud lines 1–24.

b. Discuss what you think Shylock and Bassanio are trying to achieve in these lines. For example, Shylock might want to find out if he should make the loan or he might want to avoid telling Bassanio whether he will make the loan. Write down what you decide for the character you are playing. That is the character's objective.

c. Now read aloud lines 1–24 again. Every time your character says something that helps them to achieve their objective from task b, tick beside the objective.

d. Look back over lines 1–24, remembering the points at which you added ticks. Write down the tactics you think Shylock and Bassanio used at those points. Use the photo on this page to help you.

Glossary

1 **ducats** Venetian gold coins
4 **bound** legally bound to pay back
6 **stead** assist
6 **pleasure** oblige
13 **sufficient** enough security
14 **in supposition** uncertain
14 **argosy** merchant ship
15 **the Rialto** Venetian stock exchange
20 **notwithstanding** nevertheless

Key terms

Objective what a character wants to get or achieve in a scene
Tactics the methods a character uses to get what they want

Enter Bassanio with Shylock the Jew

Shylock   Three thousand ducats, well.

Bassanio   Ay, sir, for three months.

Shylock   For three months, well.

Bassanio   For the which, as I told you, Antonio shall be bound.

Shylock   Antonio shall become bound, well.   5

Bassanio   May you stead me? Will you pleasure me? Shall I know your answer?

Shylock   Three thousand ducats for three months and Antonio bound.

Bassanio   Your answer to that.

Shylock   Antonio is a good man.   10

Bassanio   Have you heard any imputation to the contrary?

Shylock   Ho, no, no, no, no. My meaning in saying he is a good man is to have you understand me that he is sufficient. Yet his means are in supposition. He hath an argosy bound to Tripolis, another to the Indies. I understand moreover, upon the Rialto, he hath a third at Mexico, a fourth for England, and other ventures he hath squandered abroad. But ships are but boards, sailors but men. There be land-rats and water-rats, water-thieves and land-thieves, I mean pirates, and then there is the peril of waters, winds and rocks. The man is, notwithstanding, sufficient. Three thousand ducats. I think I may take his bond.   15   20

Bassanio   Be assured you may.

Shylock   I will be assured I may. And that I may be assured, I will bethink me. May I speak with Antonio?

Bassanio invites Shylock to dinner with Antonio, but Shylock says he will not eat, drink or pray with the Christians. Antonio arrives and Shylock talks of his hatred of the merchant.

Bassanio and Shylock, 2008

At the time

Using the context section on page 218, find out what attitudes there were towards Judaism and usury, to help you with the activity on this page.

Key term

Aside when a character addresses a remark to the audience that other characters on the stage do not hear

Glossary

26 **habitation** the body of a pig
27 **the Nazarite** Jesus of Nazareth
32 **fawning publican** flattering tax collector
34 **low simplicity** humble foolishness
35 **gratis** interest-free
36 **usance** lending money for interest
37 **upon the hip** at a disadvantage (in wrestling)
39 **sacred nation** the Jewish people
39 **rails** rants abusively
41 **bargains** business deals
41 **thrift** profit
42 **tribe** one of the 12 tribes of Israel, from whom all Jewish people are descended
44 **debating** reckoning up
44 **store** ready money
46 **gross** whole amount
49 **furnish** supply
49 **soft** wait a moment
51 **in our mouths** we were talking about
53 **excess** interest
54 **ripe** ready, urgent
55 **possessed** informed
56 **ye would** you want

Activity 2: Exploring asides and the theme of prejudice

a. In groups, decide who will play Bassanio, Shylock and Antonio. Read aloud lines 25–43.
b. Using information you found for the 'At the time' task, discuss:
   i. which words in lines 25–43 you think reveal ethnic or religious prejudice
   ii. why you think Shakespeare gives Shylock these lines at this point.
c. Look at lines 26–30. Who do you think Shylock is talking to? Re-read lines 26–30 as if Shylock is talking to:
   i. Bassanio
   ii. himself
   iii. the audience.
d. Discuss which version, or which combination, worked best and why.
e. Prepare your version of lines 25–43 and then share this with the rest of your class.

Bassanio	If it please you to dine with us.	25

Shylock Yes, to smell pork, to eat of the habitation which your prophet
the Nazarite conjured the devil into. I will buy with you, sell with
you, talk with you, walk with you, and so following, but I will not
eat with you, drink with you, nor pray with you. What news on
the Rialto? Who is he comes here? 30

Enter Antonio

Bassanio This is Signor Antonio.

Shylock [Aside] How like a fawning publican he looks.
I hate him for he is a Christian;
But more, for that in low simplicity
He lends out money gratis and brings down 35
The rate of usance here with us in Venice.
If I can catch him once upon the hip,
I will feed fat the ancient grudge I bear him.
He hates our sacred nation, and he rails,
Even there where merchants most do congregate, 40
On me, my bargains and my well-won thrift,
Which he calls interest. Cursèd be my tribe,
If I forgive him.

Bassanio   Shylock, do you hear?

Shylock I am debating of my present store,
And by the near guess of my memory, 45
I cannot instantly raise up the gross
Of full three thousand ducats. What of that?
Tubal, a wealthy Hebrew of my tribe,
Will furnish me. But soft, how many months
Do you desire? [To Antonio] Rest you fair, good signor. 50
Your worship was the last man in our mouths.

Antonio Shylock, albeit I neither lend nor borrow
By taking nor by giving of excess,
Yet to supply the ripe wants of my friend,
I'll break a custom. [To Bassanio] Is he yet possessed 55
How much ye would?

Antonio clarifies that he wants to borrow 3000 ducats for three months. Shylock tells Antonio the Old Testament story of Jacob and the lambs (Genesis: 27 and 30). Antonio queries whether Shylock is using the story to justify the interest rates he charges on the loans that he makes.

Shylock, 2015

Key term

Subtext the underlying meaning in the script

Activity 3: Exploring subtext and the theme of value

a. In pairs, read aloud lines 67–81, swapping readers at each punctuation mark.

b. Discuss:
   i. Nowadays, banks pay interest on savings and charge interest on loans. What do you think of this?
   ii. Why do you think Antonio is opposed to interest?
   iii. Why do you think Shylock is in favour of interest?

c. Decide who will play Shylock and Antonio. The person playing Shylock reads lines 67–81, while the person playing Antonio listens politely, nodding and smiling.

d. The person playing Shylock reads lines 67–81 again, but this time Antonio can interrupt Shylock with opinions and questions at any time.

e. As Antonio, write an email to a friend that explains what Antonio thinks of Shylock at this moment. Include what Antonio values and what he thinks Shylock values.

Shylock	Ay, ay, three thousand ducats.
Antonio	And for three months.
Shylock	I had forgot, three months. [To Bassanio] You told me so. Well then, your bond. And let me see, but hear you, Methoughts you said you neither lend nor borrow 60 Upon advantage.
Antonio	I do never use it.
Shylock	When Jacob grazed his uncle Laban's sheep, This Jacob from our holy Abram was, As his wise mother wrought in his behalf, The third possessor; ay, he was the third— 65
Antonio	And what of him? Did he take interest?
Shylock	No, not take interest, not, as you would say, Directly interest. Mark what Jacob did: When Laban and himself were compromised That all the eanlings which were streaked and pied 70 Should fall as Jacob's hire, the ewes, being rank, In end of autumn turnèd to the rams, And, when the work of generation was Between these woolly breeders in the act, The skilful shepherd peeled me certain wands, 75 And in the doing of the deed of kind, He stuck them up before the fulsome ewes, Who then conceiving, did in eaning time Fall parti-coloured lambs, and those were Jacob's. This was a way to thrive, and he was blest, 80 And thrift is blessing, if men steal it not.
Antonio	This was a venture, sir, that Jacob served for, A thing not in his power to bring to pass, But swayed and fashioned by the hand of heaven. Was this inserted to make interest good? 85 Or is your gold and silver ewes and rams?
Shylock	I cannot tell, I make it breed as fast.

Antonio claims that Shylock is quoting the Bible to hide his evil nature. Shylock reminds Antonio that the merchant has publicly called him names, spat at him, kicked him and rejected him. Antonio says he is likely to do the same again.

Shylock, 2011

Activity 4: Exploring the theme of prejudice – Antonio and Shylock

a. In pairs, decide who will play Antonio and Shylock. Read aloud lines 89–121.

b. Read aloud lines 89–121 again, this time hitting your script with your hand every time your character says something about religion or religious hatred. For example, Antonio should hit his script when he says 'devil' or 'Scripture' in line 89.

c. Discuss the following:
   i. How do these characters feel about each other, and why?
   ii. What causes the strong feelings between them?
   iii. Why do you think Shakespeare gives Shylock the opportunity to say much more than Antonio?
   iv. Which character do you think makes the strongest argument?

d. Write a paragraph describing how Antonio and Shylock behave during lines 89–121, quoting the most powerful words they use and explaining how this moment contributes to the theme of prejudice.

Glossary

96 **beholding** indebted
98 **rated** berated
101 **sufferance** endurance
101 **badge** marker (At the time, Jewish people in Venice were compelled to wear a yellow O)
103 **gaberdine** long coat traditionally worn by Jews
106 **Go to** now what?
108 **void... rheum** spit
109 **foot** kick
109 **spurn** reject
109 **stranger cur** unknown dog
110 **suit** request
114 **bondsman's key** servant's tone
115 **bated** hushed

But note me, signor.

Antonio   Mark you this, Bassanio,
The devil can cite Scripture for his purpose.
An evil soul producing holy witness   90
Is like a villain with a smiling cheek,
A goodly apple rotten at the heart.
O what a goodly outside falsehood hath.

Shylock Three thousand ducats, 'tis a good round sum.
Three months from twelve, then let me see the rate.   95

Antonio Well, Shylock, shall we be beholding to you?

Shylock Signor Antonio, many a time and oft
In the Rialto you have rated me
About my moneys and my usances.
Still have I borne it with a patient shrug,   100
For sufferance is the badge of all our tribe.
You call me misbeliever, cut-throat dog,
And spit upon my Jewish gaberdine,
And all for use of that which is mine own.
Well then, it now appears you need my help.   105
Go to, then. You come to me and you say,
'Shylock, we would have moneys', you say so.
You that did void your rheum upon my beard,
And foot me as you spurn a stranger cur
Over your threshold. Moneys is your suit.   110
What should I say to you? Should I not say,
'Hath a dog money? Is it possible
A cur should lend three thousand ducats?' Or
Shall I bend low and in a bondman's key,
With bated breath and whispering humbleness,   115
Say this: 'Fair sir, you spat on me on Wednesday last,
You spurned me such a day, another time
You called me dog, and for these courtesies
I'll lend you thus much moneys'?

Antonio I am as like to call thee so again,   120
To spit on thee again, to spurn thee too.

Shylock suggests that they go to a solicitor and sign a contract for the loan, stating that the forfeit for failure to repay the debt will be a pound of Antonio's flesh. Antonio agrees, despite Bassanio's protest, confident that he will have plenty of money to repay the debt.

Antonio, Bassanio and Shylock, 2015

Activity 5: Exploring power through movement

a. In small groups, decide who will play Bassanio, Antonio and Shylock. Read aloud lines 122–150.

b. Read aloud lines 122–150 again. This time the people playing Bassanio and Antonio stand rooted to the spot. The person playing Shylock can move around the other two, using their physical presence to influence them.

c. Read the lines again, this time with Shylock rooted to the spot and the other two characters able to move wherever they like around him.

d. Discuss the following:
    i.   Who is challenging who, and when, during this section?
    ii. How could you move to show that?
    iii. Look at the photo on this page and discuss which line you think is being spoken here and why.

e. Write notes describing the blocking for lines 122–150. You could use diagrams in your description.

Glossary

124 **A... metal** an unnatural increase of money (i.e. interest)
125 **thine** your
126 **break** fails to repay
131 **doit** Dutch coin of very little value
135 **notary** solicitor
135 **seal** sign
136 **in a merry sport** for a joke
139 **the condition** the terms of the bond
140 **nominated** named
140 **equal** exact
146 **dwell... necessity** live in my need
150 **thrice** three times
154 **break his day** miss the repayment date

If thou wilt lend this money, lend it not
As to thy friends, for when did friendship take
A breed of barren metal of his friend?
But lend it rather to thine enemy,   125
Who, if he break, thou mayst with better face
Exact the penalties.

Shylock Why look you how you storm.
I would be friends with you and have your love,
Forget the shames that you have stained me with,   130
Supply your present wants and take no doit
Of usance for my moneys, and you'll not hear me.
This is kind I offer.

Bassanio   This were kindness.

Shylock This kindness will I show:
Go with me to a notary, seal me there   135
Your single bond, and in a merry sport
If you repay me not on such a day,
In such a place, such sum or sums as are
Expressed in the condition, let the forfeit
Be nominated for an equal pound   140
Of your fair flesh, to be cut off and taken
In what part of your body it pleaseth me.

Antonio Content in faith, I'll seal to such a bond,
And say there is much kindness in the Jew.

Bassanio You shall not seal to such a bond for me.   145
I'll rather dwell in my necessity.

Antonio Why, fear not, man, I will not forfeit it.
Within these two months, that's a month before
This bond expires, I do expect return
Of thrice three times the value of this bond.   150

Shylock O father Abram, what these Christians are,
Whose own hard dealings teaches them suspect
The thoughts of others. Pray you tell me this:
If he should break his day, what should I gain

Antonio and Shylock agree to meet at the solicitor's office to sign the bond. Shylock goes ahead to collect the ducats. Antonio reassures Bassanio that his ships will come home a month before the loan is due to be repaid.

Antonio and Bassanio, 2015

Activity 6: Exploring the end of a scene

a. Read aloud lines 169–172.

b. **Rhyming couplets** at the end of a speech or scene often indicate that a character has made a decision. What decision has Antonio reached here?

c. Look at the photo on this page of Antonio and Bassanio at the end of Act 1 Scene 3. Discuss:
   i. what you think has changed between Antonio and Bassanio during Act 1 Scene 3
   ii. how you think the change between them makes them feel
   iii. what your opinion is of Antonio at the end of Act 1 Scene 3.

Glossary

155 **extaction** enforcement
157 **estimable** valuable
158 **muttons** sheep
158 **beefs** cows
163 **forthwith** at once
165 **straight** immediately
166 **fearful** untrustworthy
167 **unthrifty** careless
167 **knave** scoundrel, servant
168 **Hie thee** hurry you
168 **gentle** courteous, with a **pun** on 'gentile', a non-Jewish person
169 **kind** generous; natural

Key terms

Pun a play on words
Rhyming couplet two lines of verse where the last words of each line rhyme

By the exaction of the forfeiture? 155
A pound of man's flesh taken from a man
Is not so estimable, profitable neither,
As flesh of muttons, beefs or goats. I say
To buy his favour, I extend this friendship.
If he will take it, so, if not, adieu. 160
And for my love, I pray you wrong me not.

Antonio   Yes, Shylock, I will seal unto this bond.

Shylock   Then meet me forthwith at the notary's,
Give him direction for this merry bond,
And I will go and purse the ducats straight, 165
See to my house, left in the fearful guard
Of an unthrifty knave, and presently
I'll be with you.

Exit Shylock

Antonio   Hie thee, gentle Jew.
This Hebrew will turn Christian, he grows kind.

Bassanio   I like not fair terms and a villain's mind. 170

Antonio   Come on, in this there can be no dismay.
My ships come home a month before the day.

Exeunt

Exploring Act 1

Nerissa and Portia, 2011

Activity 1: Exploring the themes of love and friendship in Act 1

a. Discuss how Shakespeare develops the themes of love and friendship in Act 1 by comparing how the following characters express their ideas about it:
   i. Antonio
   ii. Portia
   iii. Bassanio
   iv. Nerissa

b. Write a brief essay (no more than 400 words in length) entitled: 'How does Shakespeare present the themes of love and friendship in Act 1 of *The Merchant of Venice*?' You could include:
   i. the ideas you have discussed in task a, including use of language and staging
   ii. what you have noticed about how the plot is structured in Act 1
   iii. how Shakespeare encourages the audience to think about what could happen next.

Activity 2: Exploring men and women in Act 1

Work in groups.
a. Look back over Act 1 at the male characters. How does Shakespeare portray men? What words would you use to describe how the main male characters you meet in this Act:
- behave (their actions)
- speak
- think?

b. Now look back over Act 1 at the female characters. How do you think they are portrayed? What words would you use to describe how the main female characters you meet in this Act:
- behave
- speak
- think?

c. Do the male and female characters in Act 1 always act in stereotypical ways? Find quotations that illustrate the ways in which Shakespeare portrays men and women in Act 1, and suggest why these might be important.

The Prince of Morocco comes to Belmont to woo Portia. He appeals to her not to judge him by his appearance. Portia explains that her choice of husband must be through the casket challenge. Morocco asks her to lead him to the caskets.

The Prince of Morocco and Portia, 2015

Key terms

Themes the main ideas explored in a piece of literature, e.g. the themes of love and friendship, fathers and daughters, justice and mercy, prejudice, deceptive appearances and value might be considered key themes of *The Merchant of Venice*

Imagery visually descriptive language

Pun a play on words

Glossary

s.d. **Moor** North African Muslim person of Berber or Arabic descent

2 **shadowed livery** darkened uniform

2 **burnished** shining like polished metal

5 **Phoebus** god of the sun

6 **make incision** cut ourselves

8 **aspect** face

9 **feared** frightened

10 **clime** land

17 **scanted** limited

18 **hedged** protected

18–19 **yield... wife** marry that man

20 **fair** a chance; **pun** on fair-skinned

24 **scimitar** short curved sword

25 **Sophy** ruler of Persia

26 **fields** battles

26 **Solyman** sultan who fought against Persia

27 **o'erstare** outstare

Activity 1: Exploring imagery and the themes of prejudice and deceptive appearances

a. In pairs, read aloud lines 1–12, swapping readers at each punctuation mark.

b. Read line 1 again and choose the four most important words.

c. Agree gestures that could go with each of the key words to help you express what the character means.

d. Now read line 1 again, adding the gestures.

e. Work through the rest of the speech in the same way.

f. The **imagery** in Shakespeare's plays can help us understand what characters are thinking and feeling. What would you say is on the Prince's mind in this speech?

g. Write a paragraph that explains:

   i. how the imagery in lines 1–12 shows what the Prince is thinking and feeling

   ii. how what he says and does contributes to the themes of prejudice and deceptive appearances.

Act 2 | Scene 1

Enter the Prince of Morocco, a tawny Moor, all in white, and three or four
followers accordingly, with Portia, Nerissa and their train

Morocco   Mislike me not for my complexion,
The shadowed livery of the burnished sun,
To whom I am a neighbour and near bred.
Bring me the fairest creature northward born,
Where Phoebus' fire scarce thaws the icicles,   5
And let us make incision for your love,
To prove whose blood is reddest, his or mine.
I tell thee, lady, this aspect of mine
Hath feared the valiant. By my love I swear,
The best-regarded virgins of our clime   10
Have loved it too. I would not change this hue,
Except to steal your thoughts, my gentle queen.

Portia   In terms of choice I am not solely led
By nice direction of a maiden's eyes.
Besides, the lottery of my destiny   15
Bars me the right of voluntary choosing.
But if my father had not scanted me,
And hedged me by his wit to yield myself
His wife who wins me by that means I told you,
Yourself, renownèd prince, then stood as fair   20
As any comer I have looked on yet
For my affection.

Morocco   Even for that I thank you.
Therefore, I pray you lead me to the caskets
To try my fortune. By this scimitar
That slew the Sophy and a Persian prince   25
That won three fields of Sultan Solyman,
I would o'erstare the sternest eyes that look,
Outbrave the heart most daring on the earth,

Portia explains the terms of her father's will. The Prince of Morocco is still willing to take the casket challenge, so Portia invites him to choose after dinner.

The Prince of Morocco, 2008

Activity 2: Exploring a character – the Prince of Morocco

a. Read aloud lines 27–38.

b. Look at the photos of the Prince of Morocco on this page and the previous page. Using information you found for the 'At the time' task, discuss:
   i. what characteristics the Prince of Morocco is displaying
   ii. if you were Portia, how you would feel about the Prince of Morocco.

c. Create a **statue** of the Prince of Morocco as he describes himself in lines 27–38.

d. Write a character profile for the Prince of Morocco based on what you have discovered about him in Act 1 Scene 2, using quotations from the text on pages 51 and 53 in your work.

At the time

Using the context section on page 218, find out what attitudes were towards Moorish people, to help you with the activity on this page.

Key terms

Statue like a freeze-frame but usually of a single character

Freeze-frame a physical, still image created by people to represent an object, place, person or feeling

Pluck the young sucking cubs from the she-bear,
Yea, mock the lion when he roars for prey   30
To win thee, lady. But alas the while,
If Hercules and Lichas play at dice
Which is the better man, the greater throw
May turn by fortune from the weaker hand.
So is Alcides beaten by his rage,   35
And so may I, blind fortune leading me,
Miss that which one unworthier may attain,
And die with grieving.

Portia   You must take your chance,
And either not attempt to choose at all
Or swear before you choose, if you choose wrong   40
Never to speak to lady afterward
In way of marriage. Therefore be advised.

Morocco   Nor will not. Come, bring me unto my chance.

Portia   First, forward to the temple. After dinner
Your hazard shall be made.

Morocco   Good fortune then,   45
To make me blest or cursed'st among men.

Exeunt

Lancelot Gobbo, Shylock's servant, debates whether to leave his master or not. His father, who is blind, arrives and asks him the way to Shylock's house.

Lancelot Gobbo, 2011

Lancelot Gobbo, 2011

Activity 1: Exploring the function of a comic character

a. In groups, read aloud lines 1–24, swapping readers at the punctuation marks.

b. Mark the direct speech of the fiend in one colour and the speech of the conscience in another colour.

c. Decide who will play the fiend, who will play the conscience and who will play Lancelot. Read aloud lines 1–24 again, this time using the direct speech of the fiend and the conscience as if they are script and using the rest of Lancelot's words as narration.

d. Look at the photos on this page which show Lancelot and discuss:

   i. at least three things about him that make him funny

   ii. the ways in which the actor's costume and make-up add to the comic effect

   iii. why the **director** chose to have people physically playing the fiend and the conscience.

e. Write a paragraph explaining why you think Shakespeare introduces Lancelot Gobbo at this point in the play.

Key terms

Malapropism mistaken use of a word that sounds like another word but has a very different meaning

Director the person who enables the practical and creative interpretation of a dramatic script, and ultimately brings together everybody's ideas in a way that engages the audience with the play

Act 2 | Scene 2

Enter Lancelot Gobbo alone

Lancelot   Certainly my conscience will serve me to run from this Jew my
master. The fiend is at mine elbow and tempts me, saying to me,
'Gobbo, Lancelot Gobbo, good Lancelot', or 'Good Gobbo', or
'Good Lancelot Gobbo, use your legs, take the start, run away.'
My conscience says, 'No, take heed, honest Lancelot, take heed,   5
honest Gobbo', or, as aforesaid, 'Honest Lancelot Gobbo, do not
run, scorn running with thy heels.' Well, the most courageous fiend
bids me pack. 'Fia!' says the fiend, 'Away!' says the fiend, 'For the
heavens, rouse up a brave mind', says the fiend, 'and run.' Well, my
conscience, hanging about the neck of my heart, says very wisely   10
to me, 'My honest friend Lancelot, being an honest man's son', or
rather an honest woman's son, for indeed my father did something
smack, something grow to, he had a kind of taste – well, my
conscience says, 'Lancelot, budge not.' 'Budge,' says the fiend.
'Budge not,' says my conscience. 'Conscience,' say I, 'you counsel   15
well. Fiend,' say I, 'you counsel well.' To be ruled by my conscience,
I should stay with the Jew my master, who, God bless the mark, is
a kind of devil, and to run away from the Jew, I should be ruled
by the fiend, who, saving your reverence, is the devil himself.
Certainly the Jew is the very devil incarnation, and in my   20
conscience, my conscience is a kind of hard conscience to offer to
counsel me to stay with the Jew; the fiend gives the more friendly
counsel. I will run, fiend. My heels are at your commandment. I
will run.

Enter Old Gobbo, with a basket

Gobbo   Master young man, you, I pray you which is the way to Master   25
Jew's?

Lancelot   [Aside] O heavens, this is my true-begotten father, who, being
more than sand-blind, high-gravel-blind, knows me not. I will try

Old Gobbo and Lancelot Gobbo, 2008

Activity 2: Exploring blindness and the theme of deceptive appearances

a. In pairs, decide who will play Lancelot and Gobbo. Read aloud lines 30–58.

b. Read aloud the lines again, but this time listen carefully to your partner and, before you read your next lines, repeat out loud a significant phrase that your partner said. Use what you heard to help you deliver your own lines more convincingly.

c. Using information you found for the 'At the time' task, discuss:
   i. which character you think is in charge in this scene
   ii. why Shakespeare chooses to make Old Gobbo a blind character
   iii. how the inclusion of Old Gobbo helps to make this scene funny
   iv. how lines 30–58 develop the theme of deceptive appearances.

d. Write down what your character would be thinking during lines 30–58, and why. Share your work with your partner.

e. Write a paragraph that explains why you think Shakespeare included lines 30–58 in the play, including why he makes Old Gobbo a blind character and how this moment contributes to the theme of deceptive appearances.

At the time

Using the context section on page 217, find out what the Elizabethans believed about fate, to help you with the activity on this page.

Glossary

30 **Master** i.e. Lancelot's master, Shylock

33–34 **of no hand** neither left nor right

35 **sonties** saints

35 **hit** find

38 **raise the waters** provoke tears

39 **master** gentleman

40 **well to live** malapropism for 'well-to-do'

41 **a** he

44 *ergo* therefore

47 **father** respectful way of addressing an old man

49 **Sisters Three** the fates, goddesses who spin, measure and cut the thread of a person's life

53 **hovel-post** doorpost of a poor home

confusions with him.

| Gobbo | Master young gentleman, I pray you which is the way to Master Jew's? | 30 |

| Lancelot | Turn upon your right hand at the next turning, but at the next turning of all, on your left, marry, at the very next turning, turn of no hand, but turn down indirectly to the Jew's house. | |

| Gobbo | By God's sonties, 'twill be a hard way to hit. Can you tell me whether one Lancelot, that dwells with him, dwell with him or no? | 35 |

| Lancelot | Talk you of young Master Lancelot? [Aside] Mark me now, now will I raise the waters. Talk you of young Master Lancelot? | |

| Gobbo | No master, sir, but a poor man's son. His father, though I say it, is an honest exceeding poor man and, God be thanked, well to live. | 40 |

| Lancelot | Well, let his father be what a will, we talk of young Master Lancelot. | |

| Gobbo | Your worship's friend and Lancelot. | |

| Lancelot | But I pray you, *ergo* old man, *ergo* I beseech you, talk you of young Master Lancelot? | 45 |

| Gobbo | Of Lancelot, and it please your mastership. | |

| Lancelot | *Ergo* Master Lancelot. Talk not of Master Lancelot, father, for the young gentleman, according to fates and destinies and such odd sayings, the Sisters Three and such branches of learning, is indeed deceased, or as you would say in plain terms, gone to heaven. | 50 |

| Gobbo | Marry, God forbid! The boy was the very staff of my age, my very prop. | |

| Lancelot | Do I look like a cudgel or a hovel-post, a staff or a prop? Do you know me, father? | |

| Gobbo | Alack the day, I know you not, young gentleman, but I pray you tell me, is my boy, God rest his soul, alive or dead? | 55 |

| Lancelot | Do you not know me, father? | |

| Gobbo | Alack, sir, I am sand-blind. I know you not. | |

Lancelot reveals to Old Gobbo that he is his son. Old Gobbo has brought a present for Shylock, but Lancelot tells his father that he wants to leave his master to serve Bassanio. Along comes Bassanio, with followers.

Lancelot Gobbo, Old Gobbo, Balthasar and Bassanio, 2008

Key terms

Blocking the movements agreed for **staging** a scene

Staging the process of selecting, adapting and developing the stage space in which a play will be performed

Glossary

60 **it... child** Lancelot inverts the proverb 'It is a wise child that knows his own father'

71 **thou** you (respectful form)

74 **fill-horse** carthorse (which 'fills' the shafts of a cart)

75 **backward** inward; shorter

76 **of** on

79 **'gree** agree

80 **for... part** as far as I am concerned

80 **set... rest** staked everything on

81 **ground** distance

82 **very** absolute

82 **halter** hangman's noose

83 **tell... ribs** count every one of my ribs with your fingers

84 **Give... present** give your present on my behalf

85 **rare new liveries** magnificent new uniforms

87 **a Jew** i.e. a villain

Activity 3: Exploring the action

a. In groups, decide who will play Lancelot, Gobbo, Bassanio, Leonardo and followers. Read aloud lines 71–88. Note that Lancelot says, 'Here comes the man' in lines 86–87. This is an action clue. You will have to decide whether Lancelot is speaking to his father, Bassanio and his followers, or to all of them.

b. You are now going to agree the movements, or **blocking**, for lines 71–88. On your feet, work out the blocking for lines 71–88, using the action clues. Remember that Old Gobbo is blind.

c. If you need inspiration, use the photo on this page to help you.

Lancelot	Nay, indeed if you had your eyes you might fail of the knowing me: it is a wise father that knows his own child. Well, old man, I will tell you news of your son. Give me your blessing. Truth will come to light, murder cannot be hid long, a man's son may, but in the end truth will out.
Gobbo	Pray you, sir, stand up. I am sure you are not Lancelot, my boy.
Lancelot	Pray you let's have no more fooling about it, but give me your blessing. I am Lancelot, your boy that was, your son that is, your child that shall be.
Gobbo	I cannot think you are my son.
Lancelot	I know not what I shall think of that. But I am Lancelot, the Jew's man, and I am sure Margery your wife is my mother.
Gobbo	Her name is Margery, indeed. I'll be sworn, if thou be Lancelot, thou art mine own flesh and blood. Lord worshipped might he be, what a beard hast thou got! Thou hast got more hair on thy chin than Dobbin my fill-horse has on his tail.
Lancelot	It should seem, then, that Dobbin's tail grows backward. I am sure he had more hair of his tail than I have of my face when I last saw him.
Gobbo	Lord, how art thou changed. How dost thou and thy master agree? I have brought him a present. How 'gree you now?
Lancelot	Well, well. But for mine own part, as I have set up my rest to run away, so I will not rest till I have run some ground. My master's a very Jew. Give him a present? Give him a halter! I am famished in his service. You may tell every finger I have with my ribs. Father, I am glad you are come. Give me your present to one Master Bassanio, who, indeed, gives rare new liveries. If I serve not him, I will run as far as God has any ground. O rare fortune! Here comes the man. To him, father, for I am a Jew if I serve the Jew any longer.
	Enter Bassanio, with Leonardo and followers
Bassanio	You may do so, but let it be so hasted that supper be ready at

Old Gobbo and Lancelot Gobbo, 2011

Key term

Pace the speed at which someone speaks

Glossary

90–91 **put… making** make sure the uniforms are made

91 **desire** request

91 **anon** shortly

95 **Gramercy** many thanks

95 **aught** anything

99 **infection** malapropism for 'affection'

102 **saving… reverence** if you will allow me to say this, sir

103 **cater-cousins** good friends that eat together

105 **doth** does

106 **fruitify** malapropism for 'notify'/'fructify' (bear fruit)

108 **suit** request

109 **impertinent** malapropism for 'pertinent', meaning relevant

114 **defect** malapropism for 'effect'

117 **preferred** recommended; promoted

Activity 4: Exploring pace

a. In groups, decide who will play Lancelot, Gobbo and Bassanio. Read aloud lines 93–115.

b. Now stand up and try playing different versions of lines 93–115:

   i. In the first version, leave a two-second pause before each character speaks.

   ii. In the second version, interrupt the previous speaker with your line whenever there is a dash at the end of their line.

c. Discuss which of these versions you prefer and why.

d. Read aloud lines 93–115 again, this time varying the **pace** of your speech according to how you think they should be played.

e. Write a paragraph arguing what you think the pace of lines 93–115 should be, and explaining the ways in which the pace of the lines adds to the comic effect.

the farthest by five of the clock. See these letters delivered, put 90
the liveries to making, and desire Gratiano to come anon to my
lodging.

Exit one of his followers

Lancelot   To him, father.

Gobbo   God bless your worship.

Bassanio   Gramercy, wouldst thou aught with me? 95

Gobbo   Here's my son, sir, a poor boy—

Lancelot   Not a poor boy, sir, but the rich Jew's man, that would, sir, as my
father shall specify—

Gobbo   He hath a great infection, sir, as one would say, to serve—

Lancelot   Indeed, the short and the long is, I serve the Jew and have a desire, 100
as my father shall specify—

Gobbo   His master and he, saving your worship's reverence, are scarce
cater-cousins—

Lancelot   To be brief, the very truth is that the Jew, having done me wrong,
doth cause me, as my father, being, I hope, an old man, shall 105
frutify unto you—

Gobbo   I have here a dish of doves that I would bestow upon your
worship, and my suit is—

Lancelot   In very brief, the suit is impertinent to myself, as your worship
shall know by this honest old man, and though I say it, though old 110
man, yet poor man, my father—

Bassanio   One speak for both. What would you?

Lancelot   Serve you, sir.

Gobbo   That is the very defect of the matter, sir.

Bassanio   I know thee well, thou hast obtained thy suit. 115
Shylock thy master spoke with me this day,
And hath preferred thee, if it be preferment

Bassanio instructs Lancelot to go and tell Shylock that he is leaving his service. Bassanio reveals that he is giving a feast that night for his best friends. Gratiano arrives.

Lancelot Gobbo, 2015

Key terms

Improvise make up in the moment
Offstage the part of the stage the audience cannot see
Motivation a person's reason for doing something

Glossary

120 **old proverb** i.e. 'the grace of God is enough'
120 **parted** divided
124–125 **inquire... out** find out where I live
126 **guarded** decorated with braid
129 **table** palm of the hand
129 **book** the Bible
130 **Go to** come on
130 **line of life** the line on the palm of the hand believed to tell the story of a person's life
130 **trifle** insignificant amount
132 **simple coming-in** only a beginning
132 **'scape** escape
133 **thrice** three times
134 **Fortune** fate; luck
135 **gear** business
136 **the twinkling** the twinkling of an eye
138 **bestowed** stored (i.e. on his ship bound for Belmont)
141 **herein** in this matter

Did you know?

Actors sometimes find it useful to **improvise** events that are mentioned or described in the play but not seen on stage, such as Lancelot's conversation with Shylock.

Activity 5: Exploring an offstage event

a. Read aloud lines 123–125 and lines 135–136.
b. Imagine the conversation in which Lancelot tells Shylock that he is leaving and why.
c. In pairs, decide who will play Lancelot and Shylock. Improvise their conversation.
d. Write the script of this imagined conversation in modern English, using no more than ten lines.
e. In pairs, perform your script, then give feedback to other pairs on their performances. What have you learned about Lancelot's **motivation** through this exploration?

	To leave a rich Jew's service, to become	
	The follower of so poor a gentleman.	
Lancelot	The old proverb is very well parted between my master	120
	Shylock and you, sir: you have the grace of God, sir, and he hath	
	enough.	
Bassanio	Thou speak'st it well. Go, father, with thy son.	
	Take leave of thy old master and inquire	
	My lodging out. [To a follower] Give him a livery	125
	More guarded than his fellows'. See it done.	
Lancelot	Father, in. I cannot get a service, no, I have ne'er a tongue in my	
	head. [Looks at palm of his hand] Well, if any man in Italy have a	
	fairer table which doth offer to swear upon a book, I shall have	
	good fortune. Go to, here's a simple line of life, here's a small trifle	130
	of wives. Alas, fifteen wives is nothing. Eleven widows and nine	
	maids is a simple coming-in for one man, and then to 'scape	
	drowning thrice, and to be in peril of my life with the edge of a	
	feather-bed. Here are simple 'scapes. Well, if Fortune be a woman,	
	she's a good wench for this gear. Father, come. I'll take my leave	135
	of the Jew in the twinkling.	

Exeunt Lancelot with Old Gobbo

Bassanio	I pray thee good Leonardo, think on this.	
	These things being bought and orderly bestowed,	
	Return in haste, for I do feast tonight	
	My best-esteemed acquaintance. Hie thee, go.	140
Leonardo	My best endeavours shall be done herein.	

Enter Gratiano

Gratiano	Where's your master?	
Leonardo	Yonder, sir, he walks.	

Exit Leonardo

Gratiano	Signor Bassanio.	
Bassanio	Gratiano.	

Gratiano asks Bassanio if he can go with him to Belmont. Bassanio agrees, but warns Gratiano to behave himself. They look forward to partying with their friends.

Bassanio and Gratiano, 2015

Activity 6: Exploring the themes of love and friendship – Bassanio and Gratiano

a. In pairs, decide who will play Gratiano and Bassanio. Read aloud lines 144–173.
b. Stand a few steps apart. To help you understand more about the characters, their relationship and their motives, read lines 144–173 again. This time, as you speak and listen, you should keep choosing between the following movements:
   - Take a step towards the other character.
   - Take a step away from the other character.
   - Turn towards the other character.
   - Turn away from the other character.
   - Stand still.

   Try to make instinctive choices rather than planning what to do.
c. Discuss what friendship means to these two characters.
d. Write a summary of what happens in lines 144–173 from the point of view of the character you have been playing, including ideas about love and friendship. Use quotations to explain what happens. You could style this as a blog or an interview.

Glossary

149 **Parts** qualities
149 **become thee** suit you
153 **allay** calm
153 **modesty** restraint
154 **skipping** frivolous
155 **misconstered** misunderstood
157 **sober habit** sensible behaviour; clothes
160 **hood** cover
163 **studied... ostent** practised in appearing solemn
164 **grandam** grandmother
165 **bearing** behaviour
167 **were** would be a
169 **suit of mirth** party clothes; entertaining conduct

Gratiano   I have a suit to you.

Bassanio   You have obtained it.   145

Gratiano   You must not deny me. I must go with you to Belmont.

Bassanio   Why then you must. But hear thee, Gratiano,
Thou art too wild, too rude and bold of voice,
Parts that become thee happily enough
And in such eyes as ours appear not faults,   150
But where they are not known, why, there they show
Something too liberal. Pray thee take pain
To allay with some cold drops of modesty
Thy skipping spirit, lest through thy wild behaviour
I be misconstered in the place I go to,   155
And lose my hopes.

Gratiano   Signor Bassanio, hear me.
If I do not put on a sober habit,
Talk with respect and swear but now and then,
Wear prayer-books in my pocket, look demurely,
Nay more, while grace is saying, hood mine eyes   160
Thus with my hat, and sigh and say 'amen',
Use all the observance of civility,
Like one well studied in a sad ostent
To please his grandam, never trust me more.

Bassanio   Well, we shall see your bearing.   165

Gratiano   Nay, but I bar tonight. You shall not gauge me
By what we do tonight.

Bassanio   No, that were pity.
I would entreat you rather to put on
Your boldest suit of mirth, for we have friends
That purpose merriment. But fare you well.   170
I have some business.

Gratiano   And I must to Lorenzo and the rest,
But we will visit you at suppertime.

Exeunt

Jessica says goodbye to Lancelot. She reveals to the audience that she is planning to convert to Christianity and marry Lorenzo.

Jessica, 2011

Activity 1: Exploring the theme of fathers and daughters, and predicting the plot

a. In groups, read aloud lines 15–20, swapping readers at each punctuation mark.

b. Decide which you think are the most important words in lines 15–20. Choose at least four words. What image do they create?

c. Agree gestures that could go with each of the key words you have chosen. Use gestures that help you to express exactly what the character means.

d. Using information you found for the 'At the time' task and the clues in the text on the opposite page, work out in detail what you think Jessica's plan could be.

e. Write a speech for Jessica in modern English, in which she explains the plan to Lancelot, including how she feels about her father and what her plan means for her as a daughter.

f. In your group, one person should read aloud the speech you have written for Jessica as if they are that character. The rest of the group should act out the plan, playing the other characters that she mentions, as required. The action should be exaggerated and clear, in the style of a silent film.

At the time

Using the context section on page 222, find out how society expected women to behave, to help you with the activity on this page.

Did you know?

Actors try to play every moment of the play as if it is the first time it has happened and as if anything could happen next in order to keep the action believable.

Glossary

10 **Adieu** goodbye (French)

10 **exhibit** express, malapropism for 'inhibit'

11 **get thee** steal you

15 **heinous** monstrous

18 **manners** behaviour; character

Act 2 | Scene 3

Enter Jessica and Lancelot

Jessica   I am sorry thou wilt leave my father so.
Our house is hell, and thou, a merry devil,
Didst rob it of some taste of tediousness.
But fare thee well. There is a ducat for thee.
And, Lancelot, soon at supper shalt thou see   5
Lorenzo, who is thy new master's guest.
Give him this letter. Do it secretly.
And so farewell. I would not have my father
See me talk with thee.

Lancelot   Adieu. Tears exhibit my tongue, most beautiful pagan, most sweet   10
Jew. If a Christian do not play the knave and get thee, I am much
deceived. But adieu. These foolish drops do somewhat drown my
manly spirit. Adieu.

Exit Lancelot

Jessica   Farewell, good Lancelot.
Alack, what heinous sin is it in me   15
To be ashamed to be my father's child.
But though I am a daughter to his blood,
I am not to his manners. O Lorenzo,
If thou keep promise, I shall end this strife,
Become a Christian and thy loving wife.   20

Exit

Lorenzo and his friends plan what they will do that evening, when Lancelot brings a letter from Jessica. Lorenzo asks Lancelot to give Jessica the message that he will come for her that night. Lancelot goes to find Jessica at Shylock's house.

Gratiano, Salarino and Lorenzo, 2011

Lorenzo and Lancelot Gobbo, 2008

Lancelot Gobbo and Lorenzo, 2015

At the time

Using the context section on page 214, find out about the theatres that Shakespeare's plays were first performed in, to help you with the activity on this page.

Activity 1: Exploring Shakespeare's theatre

a. In groups, decide who will play Gratiano, Lorenzo, Salarino, Solanio and Lancelot. Read aloud lines 1–19.

b. Look at the photos on this page, which show moments from lines 1–19 in three different productions. Using ideas from the photos and information you found for the 'At the time' task, discuss the following:

   i. Where on stage would you place the first part of the scene (lines 1–9) and why?

   ii. The **stage direction** in line 9 is from the first published version of the play. Where do you think Lancelot should enter the stage, and why?

   iii. At what point exactly do you think Lancelot gives Lorenzo the letter?

   iv. What do you think Lorenzo gives to Lancelot in line 18, and why?

   v. How would you stage lines 1–19?

c. Draw or write notes to describe what you have discussed in task b.

Key term

Stage direction an instruction in the text of a play, e.g. indicating which characters enter and exit a scene

Act 2 | Scene 4

Enter Gratiano, Lorenzo, Salarino and Solanio

Lorenzo   Nay, we will slink away in suppertime,
Disguise us at my lodging and return
All in an hour.

Gratiano   We have not made good preparation.

Salarino   We have not spoke us yet of torchbearers.   5

Solanio   'Tis vile, unless it may be quaintly ordered,
And better in my mind not undertook.

Lorenzo   'Tis now but four of clock. We have two hours
To furnish us.

Enter Lancelot, with a letter

Friend Lancelot, what's the news?

Lancelot   And it shall please you to break up this, it shall seem to signify.   10

Lorenzo   I know the hand. In faith, 'tis a fair hand,
And whiter than the paper it writ on
Is the fair hand that writ.

Gratiano   Love-news, in faith.

Lancelot   By your leave, sir.

Lorenzo   Whither goest thou?   15

Lancelot   Marry, sir, to bid my old master the Jew to sup tonight with my
new master the Christian.

Lorenzo   Hold here, take this. Tell gentle Jessica
I will not fail her. Speak it privately.

Exit Lancelot

Salarino and Solanio agree to meet Lorenzo and Gratiano later, then go to get ready for the masque. Gratiano asks Lorenzo if the letter was from Jessica, and Lorenzo reveals Jessica's plan.

Gratiano and Lorenzo, 2011

Activity 2: Exploring Jessica's plan and the themes of fathers and daughters, and prejudice

a. In groups, read aloud lines 28–31, swapping readers at each punctuation mark.
b. Discuss what plan Jessica has proposed in the letter.
c. Write down the plan as a sequence of events.
d. Create a freeze-frame for each of the events in the plan.
e. Choose a line from lines 28–31 to go with each of your freeze-frames.
f. Share your version with the rest of the class.
g. Discuss how Jessica's plan helps to develop the theme of fathers and daughters.
h. Read aloud lines 32–38, swapping readers at each punctuation mark.
i. Write a paragraph that explains how Lorenzo's attitude to the plan helps to develop the theme of prejudice.

Glossary

22 **provided of** supplied with
23 **straight** immediately
25 **some hour hence** in about an hour
28 **I... all** I must tell you everything
30 **she is furnished with** has in her possession
31 **page's suit** male servant's clothes
33 **gentle** kind, pun on 'gentile', a non-Jewish person
34 **foot** path
36 **issue to** the child of
36 **faithless** without faith; dishonest
37 **peruse** study

Did you know?

Actors listen carefully when they are exploring a scene to make sure they are using all the evidence in the text.

	Go, gentlemen,	20
	Will you prepare you for this masque tonight?	
	I am provided of a torchbearer.	

Salarino Ay, marry, I'll be gone about it straight.

Solanio And so will I.

Lorenzo   Meet me and Gratiano
At Gratiano's lodging some hour hence.   25

Salarino 'Tis good we do so.

Exeunt Salarino and Solanio

Gratiano Was not that letter from fair Jessica?

Lorenzo I must needs tell thee all. She hath directed
How I shall take her from her father's house,
What gold and jewels she is furnished with,   30
What page's suit she hath in readiness.
If e'er the Jew her father come to heaven,
It will be for his gentle daughter's sake;
And never dare misfortune cross her foot,
Unless she do it under this excuse,   35
That she is issue to a faithless Jew.
Come, go with me, peruse this as thou goest.
Fair Jessica shall be my torchbearer.

Exeunt

Lancelot tries to persuade Shylock to go to supper at Bassanio's house. Shylock calls his daughter in order to give her the keys to his house.

Shylock and Jessica, 2011

Activity 1: Exploring a character — Shylock

a. In groups, read aloud lines 11–18, swapping readers at the end of each line.

b. Read the lines again, but this time listen carefully and, before you read your lines, repeat out loud the last few words that the previous speaker said. Use those words to help you deliver your own lines more convincingly.

c. What do you think Shylock's fears are? Make a freeze-frame that shows Shylock's fears.

d. Bring your freeze-frame to life by speaking lines 11–18. As you speak, show what is being described by Shylock.

e. Imagine you are Shylock. In modern English, write an anonymous blog expressing your fears and what is causing them.

Glossary

3 **gourmandize** eat excessively

5 **rend apparel out** wear out your clothes

8 **wont** accustomed

11 **bid forth** invited out

12 **wherefore** why

14 **upon** i.e. at the expense of

15 **prodigal** wasteful

16 **to** after

18 **tonight** last night

20 **reproach** malapropism for 'approach'

23–24 **fell a-bleeding** bled (nose bleeds were thought to be bad omens)

24 **Black Monday** Easter Monday

25 **Ash Wednesday** the first day of Lent (Lancelot is talking nonsense)

Act 2 | Scene 5

Enter Shylock and Lancelot, his man that was

Shylock Well, thou shall see, thy eyes shall be thy judge,
The difference of old Shylock and Bassanio.
What, Jessica! Thou shalt not gormandize
As thou hast done with me. What, Jessica!
And sleep and snore, and rend apparel out.   5
Why, Jessica, I say!

Lancelot   Why, Jessica!

Shylock Who bids thee call? I do not bid thee call.

Lancelot Your worship was wont to tell me I could do nothing without
bidding.

Enter Jessica

Jessica Call you? What is your will?   10

Shylock I am bid forth to supper, Jessica.
There are my keys. But wherefore should I go?
I am not bid for love, they flatter me.
But yet I'll go in hate, to feed upon
The prodigal Christian. Jessica, my girl,   15
Look to my house. I am right loath to go.
There is some ill a-brewing towards my rest,
For I did dream of money-bags tonight.

Lancelot I beseech you, sir, go. My young master doth expect your
reproach.   20

Shylock So do I his.

Lancelot And they have conspired together. I will not say you shall see a
masque, but if you do, then it was not for nothing that my nose fell
a-bleeding on Black Monday last at six o'clock i'th'morning, falling
out that year on Ash Wednesday was four year, in the afternoon.   25

Shylock still has doubts, but he decides to go to Bassanio's for dinner, instructing Jessica to lock herself in. Lancelot secretly delivers Lorenzo's message to Jessica before going on ahead to Bassanio's house. Jessica is left alone in charge of the keys to Shylock's house.

Jessica and Shylock, 2008

At the time

Using the context section on page 221, find out how children were supposed to behave towards their parents, to help you with the activity on this page.

Glossary

28 **wry-necked fife** a pipe played sideways, giving the musician a twisted neck

29 **casements** windows

31 **varnished faces** painted masks

33 **foppery** foolishness

34 **Jacob's staff** biblical, Jacob owned nothing except a staff but became a rich man

35 **forth** away from home

40 **worth a Jewès eye** proverbial, something very valuable (old pronunciation of 'Jew's')

41 **Hagar's offspring** biblical, Abraham cast out Hagar and her child

43 **patch** fool

45 **wild-cat** nocturnal cat that sleeps all day

45 **Drones** non-worker bees

51 **Fast... find** proverbial, keep what you've got and you'll soon get more

Did you know?

Imagining what else could have happened at a turning point in a play helps an actor to consider the consequences of the choice their character makes and the importance of how and why they make that choice.

Activity 2: Exploring a turning point and the theme of fathers and daughters

a. In groups, decide who will play Shylock, Jessica and Lancelot. Read aloud lines 36–54.

b. Discuss why you think Jessica lies to her father in line 42.

c. Shylock makes a decision at this point in the play to leave his daughter in charge of his house and go to Bassanio's for supper. Imagine that instead of leaving, he chooses to stay in. What do you think might happen next?

d. In groups, using information you found for the 'At the time' task, create a series of three freeze-frames that tell the story in task c.

Shylock	What, are there masques? Hear you me, Jessica:
	Lock up my doors, and when you hear the drum
	And the vile squealing of the wry-necked fife,
	Clamber not you up to the casements then,
	Nor thrust your head into the public street 30
	To gaze on Christian fools with varnished faces,
	But stop my house's ears, I mean my casements.
	Let not the sound of shallow foppery enter
	My sober house. By Jacob's staff I swear
	I have no mind of feasting forth tonight, 35
	But I will go. Go you before me, sirrah,
	Say I will come.
Lancelot	I will go before, sir.
	[Aside to Jessica] Mistress, look out at window, for all this,
	There will come a Christian by,
	Will be worth a Jewès eye. 40

Exit Lancelot

Shylock	What says that fool of Hagar's offspring, ha?
Jessica	His words were 'Farewell mistress', nothing else.
Shylock	The patch is kind enough, but a huge feeder,
	Snail-slow in profit, but he sleeps by day
	More than the wild-cat. Drones hive not with me, 45
	Therefore I part with him, and part with him
	To one that I would have him help to waste
	His borrowed purse. Well, Jessica, go in.
	Perhaps I will return immediately.
	Do as I bid you, shut doors after you. 50
	Fast bind, fast find;
	A proverb never stale in thrifty mind.

Exit Shylock

Jessica	Farewell, and if my fortune be not crossed,
	I have a father, you a daughter lost.

Exit

The masque is happening in the street outside Shylock's house. Gratiano and Salarino come to meet Lorenzo under Jessica's window as arranged, but Lorenzo is late. Gratiano entertains Salarino with his theories about new love.

Activity 1: Exploring antithesis

a. In pairs, read aloud lines 9–20, swapping readers sentence by sentence.

b. Using the glossary, **paraphrase** lines 9–20.

c. List all the images containing opposites that are mentioned in these lines.

d. Using exaggerated gestures, one of you should show each positive image mentioned and the other show how this image is changed to a negative. For example, for lines 9–10, one of you could show someone rising full from a feast and the other show someone sitting down hungry.

e. Write a paragraph that explains how Shakespeare's use of antithesis in lines 9–20 helps to make what Gratiano says funny.

Gratiano and Servant, 2008

Did you know?

Actors sometimes explore **antithesis** in rehearsals by physically acting out the opposing concepts that are contained in their lines. They do this so that they can feel the tension between the opposites as they speak.

Key terms

Antithesis bringing two opposing concepts or ideas together, e.g. *hot and cold, love and hate, loud and quiet*

Paraphrase put a line or section of text into your own words

Act 2 | Scene 6

Enter the Masquers, Gratiano and Salarino

Gratiano   This is the penthouse under which Lorenzo
Desired us to make a stand.

Salarino   His hour is almost past.

Gratiano   And it is marvel he out-dwells his hour,
For lovers ever run before the clock.   5

Salarino   O ten times faster Venus' pigeons fly
To seal love's bonds new-made, than they are wont
To keep obligèd faith unforfeited.

Gratiano   That ever holds. Who riseth from a feast
With that keen appetite that he sits down?   10
Where is the horse that doth untread again
His tedious measures with the unbated fire
That he did pace them first? All things that are,
Are with more spirit chasèd than enjoyed.
How like a younger or a prodigal   15
The scarfèd bark puts from her native bay,
Hugged and embracèd by the strumpet wind.
How like a prodigal doth she return,
With over-withered ribs and ragged sails,
Lean, rent and beggared by the strumpet wind.   20

Enter Lorenzo

Salarino   Here comes Lorenzo. More of this hereafter.

Lorenzo   Sweet friends, your patience for my long abode;
Not I but my affairs have made you wait.
When you shall please to play the thieves for wives,
I'll watch as long for you then. Approach.   25
Here dwells my father Jew. Ho! Who's within?

Jessica, disguised in a boy's costume, comes to her window. She throws down a casket of money and jewels. Lorenzo urges her to come down so that they can run away to Bassanio's feast. Jessica says she will be straight down after she has locked up and collected some more money.

Lorenzo and Jessica, 2011

Glossary

28 **tongue** voice
36 **exchange** change (into boy's clothes)
39 **Cupid** god of desire
43 **sooth** truth
43 **light** immoral; evident; lit up
44 **office of discovery** i.e. torchbearing reveals things
46 **garnish** outfit
48 **close** secretive
48 **play the runaway** pass quickly
49 **stayed** waited
50 **gild** cover with gold
52 **by... hood** on my word
52 **gentle** dear one; gentile
53 **Beshrew** curse

At the time

Using the context section on page 214, find out what time of day Shakespeare's plays were originally performed and whether there was any stage lighting, to help you with the activity on this page.

Activity 2: Exploring the theme of value – Jessica and Lorenzo

a. In pairs, decide who will play Jessica and Lorenzo. Read aloud lines 27–51.
b. Pick out any words to do with love or money. Try saying just these words out loud to each other.
c. Look through the lines again and reduce the scene to just 12 words. These can come from anywhere in lines 27–51 and you can use whole phrases or lines.
d. Create a performance of this moment in the play, using only your 12 words, accompanied by actions and gestures. Your **tone** of voice and **body language** should clearly tell the story of what happens. Each character in the scene must respond to the words and actions of the other character.
e. Discuss what you think each character values most: love or money.
f. Using information you found for the 'At the time' task, imagine you are the director of lines 27–51. Write director's notes describing how you think these lines should be staged and why.

Key terms

Tone as in 'tone of voice'; expressing an attitude through how you say something
Body language how we communicate feelings to each other using our bodies (including facial expressions) rather than words

Enter Jessica above in boy's clothes

Jessica   Who are you? Tell me, for more certainty,
Albeit I'll swear that I do know your tongue.

Lorenzo   Lorenzo, and thy love.

Jessica   Lorenzo, certain, and my love indeed,   30
For who love I so much? And now who knows
But you, Lorenzo, whether I am yours?

Lorenzo   Heaven and thy thoughts are witness that thou art.

Jessica   Here, catch this casket, it is worth the pains.
I am glad 'tis night, you do not look on me,   35
For I am much ashamed of my exchange
But love is blind and lovers cannot see
The pretty follies that themselves commit,
For if they could, Cupid himself would blush
To see me thus transformèd to a boy.   40

Lorenzo   Descend, for you must be my torchbearer.

Jessica   What, must I hold a candle to my shames?
They in themselves, good sooth, are too too light.
Why, 'tis an office of discovery, love,
And I should be obscured.

Lorenzo   So you are, sweet,   45
Even in the lovely garnish of a boy.
But come at once,
For the close night doth play the runaway,
And we are stayed for at Bassanio's feast.

Jessica   I will make fast the doors and gild myself   50
With some more ducats, and be with you straight.

Exit Jessica above

Gratiano   Now, by my hood, a gentle and no Jew.

Lorenzo   Beshrew me but I love her heartily.
For she is wise, if I can judge of her,
And fair she is, if that mine eyes be true,   55

Jessica comes out of her father's house and goes with Lorenzo and Salarino to Bassanio's house. Antonio comes to find his friends, with news that the wind has turned and Bassanio is about to set sail for Belmont. So Gratiano abandons his party plans and hurries to join Bassanio aboard his ship.

Salarino, 2011

Gratiano, 2011

Lorenzo's follower, 2011

Activity 3: Exploring costume

a. Look at the photos on this page and page 78, which show some of the characters in Act 2 Scene 6 in their masque costumes.

b. Discuss:
   i. the time period in which this production is set
   ii. the situation that the characters are in
   iii. why you think the costume designer chose these specific costumes for these characters
   iv. the ways in which the actors' costumes add to the comic effect.

c. Look back over Act 2 Scene 6 and write a paragraph explaining why you think Shakespeare includes this scene at this point in the play.

Glossary

60 **stay** wait
65 **is come about** has changed (to the right direction for sailing)
66 **presently** immediately

And true she is, as she hath proved herself;
And therefore, like herself, wise, fair and true,
Shall she be placèd in my constant soul.

Enter Jessica

What, art thou come? On, gentlemen, away!   60
Our masquing mates by this time for us stay.

Exeunt Lorenzo, Jessica and Salarino

Enter Antonio

Antonio   Who's there?

Gratiano   Signor Antonio?

Antonio   Fie, fie, Gratiano, where are all the rest?
'Tis nine o'clock, our friends all stay for you.
No masque tonight, the wind is come about.   65
Bassanio presently will go aboard.
I have sent twenty out to seek for you.

Gratiano   I am glad on't. I desire no more delight
Than to be under sail and gone tonight.

Exeunt

In Belmont, Portia invites the Prince of Morocco to make his choice of casket.

Nerissa and Portia, 2015

At the time

Using the context section on page 218, find out about cultural diversity in Venice, to help you with the activity on this page.

Did you know?

Actors often physically explore the punctuation in a speech to help them connect with the way their character is thinking and feeling.

Activity 1: Exploring punctuation and the theme of prejudice

a. Read aloud lines 13–28. As you read, stand up on the first full stop, sit down on the next one, and then continue standing up or sitting down every time you come to an exclamation mark, full stop or question mark. When you come to a comma, stamp your foot.

b. With a partner, discuss what impact the use of punctuation has in this speech. The punctuation is an indicator of a character moving from one thought to another. What state of mind would you say the Prince of Morocco is in? How do you think he is feeling during this speech? Why might that be?

c. Write a short report explaining what you think the Prince of Morocco's state of mind is at this stage in the play. Use evidence from lines 13–28 and information you found for the 'At the time' task in your writing.

Glossary

1 **discover** reveal
2 **several** different
8 **blunt** as plain as lead
12 **withal** with it (i.e. with the casket)
19 **fair advantages** good returns
20 **dross** rubbish
22 **virgin hue** silver, the colour of the moon, ruled over by Diana, goddess of chastity
25 **weigh** assess
26 **estimation** reputation

Enter Portia with the Prince of Morocco and both their trains

Portia   Go, draw aside the curtains and discover
The several caskets to this noble prince.
Now make your choice.

Morocco   The first of gold, who this inscription bears:
'Who chooseth me shall gain what many men desire.'   5
The second, silver, which this promise carries:
'Who chooseth me shall get as much as he deserves.'
This third, dull lead, with warning all as blunt:
'Who chooseth me must give and hazard all he hath.'
How shall I know if I do choose the right?   10

Portia   The one of them contains my picture, prince.
If you choose that, then I am yours withal.

Morocco   Some god direct my judgement! Let me see.
I will survey the inscriptions back again.
What says this leaden casket?   15
'Who chooseth me must give and hazard all he hath.'
Must give, for what? For lead? Hazard for lead?
This casket threatens. Men that hazard all
Do it in hope of fair advantages.
A golden mind stoops not to shows of dross,   20
I'll then nor give nor hazard aught for lead.
What says the silver with her virgin hue?
'Who chooseth me shall get as much as he deserves.'
As much as he deserves. Pause there, Morocco,
And weigh thy value with an even hand.   25
If thou beest rated by thy estimation,
Thou dost deserve enough, and yet enough
May not extend so far as to the lady.
And yet to be afeard of my deserving

The Prince of Morocco chooses the golden casket, unlocks it and discovers a skull inside.

Did you know?

In Elizabethan times, the audience would say they were going to 'hear' rather than see a play in the theatre and the audience were used to listening for prolonged periods of time.

Glossary

30 **disabling** belittling

36 **graved** engraved

41 **Hyrcanian deserts** notoriously wild region of Persia

44 **watery kingdom** the sea

44 **head** waves

46 **spirits** courageus men

50 **base** unworthy, pun on 'base metal'

51 **rib** enclose (i.e. like a ribcage)

51 **cerecloth** shroud

51 **obscure** dark

52 **immured** contained; imprisoned

53 **undervalued to tried** less in value compared with pure

57 **insculped** engraved

63 **carrion Death** death's-head skull

Activity 2: Exploring the themes of deceptive appearances and value – the Prince of Morocco

a. In pairs, read aloud lines 32–60, swapping readers at each punctuation mark.

b. Read the first sentence aloud and decide which you think are the most important words. Choose at least six words.

c. Create gestures that could go with each of the key words you have chosen. Use gestures that help you to express exactly what the character means.

d. Now read the sentence again, making the gestures.

e. Work through the rest of the speech in the same way.

f. Look back over lines 13–60. Discuss:

   i. why you think Shakespeare gives the Prince of Morocco such a long and detailed speech

   ii. the ways in which the language of this speech engages the audience

   iii. how this speech helps you to understand the themes of deceptive appearances and value.

Were but a weak disabling of myself.   30
As much as I deserve? Why, that's the lady.
I do in birth deserve her, and in fortunes,
In graces and in qualities of breeding,
But more than these, in love I do deserve.
What if I strayed no farther, but chose here?   35
Let's see once more this saying graved in gold:
'Who chooseth me shall gain what many men desire.'
Why, that's the lady, all the world desires her.
From the four corners of the earth they come,
To kiss this shrine, this mortal breathing saint.   40
The Hyrcanian deserts and the vasty wilds
Of wide Arabia are as throughfares now
For princes to come view fair Portia.
The watery kingdom, whose ambitious head
Spits in the face of heaven, is no bar   45
To stop the foreign spirits, but they come,
As o'er a brook, to see fair Portia.
One of these three contains her heavenly picture.
Is't like that lead contains her? 'Twere damnation
To think so base a thought; it were too gross   50
To rib her cerecloth in the obscure grave.
Or shall I think in silver she's immured,
Being ten times undervalued to tried gold?
O sinful thought. Never so rich a gem
Was set in worse than gold! They have in England   55
A coin that bears the figure of an angel
Stamped in gold, but that's insculped upon;
But here an angel in a golden bed
Lies all within. Deliver me the key.
Here do I choose, and thrive I as I may.   60

Portia   There, take it, Prince, and if my form lie there,
Then I am yours.

Morocco unlocks the gold casket

Morocco   O hell! What have we here?
A carrion Death, within whose empty eye

The Prince of Morocco reads a scroll which is in the golden casket, telling him he has chosen wrongly. He leaves. Portia hopes that anyone else like him will fail the challenge.

Key term

Rhyming couplet two lines of verse where the last words of each line rhyme

The Prince of Morocco, 2015

Activity 3: Exploring a character — Portia

a. Look back through Act 2 Scene 7 to remind yourself of what happens.
b. Discuss the following:
    i.   How does the Prince of Morocco feel when he first enters the scene? Is there any change in this emotion by the time he leaves? Look back at the activity on page 52. What did you find out about the Prince of Morocco?
    ii. In line 79, which meaning of the word 'complexion' do you think Portia is using? Use the glossary above to help you.
    iii. Who do you think Portia addresses her final **rhyming couplet** (lines 78–79) to? How might she deliver these lines? What does this reveal about her?
c. Look at the photo on this page. Which moment in Act 2 Scene 7 would you say this was, and why?
d. Look back at the activity on page 34 and review the opinion you formed of Portia then.
e. Write a character profile for Portia based on what you have discovered about her by the end of Act 2 Scene 7.

There is a written scroll. I'll read the writing.
    'All that glisters is not gold,   65
    Often have you heard that told.
    Many a man his life hath sold
    But my outside to behold.
    Gilded tombs do worms enfold.
    Had you been as wise as bold,   70
    Young in limbs, in judgement old,
    Your answer had not been inscrolled.
    Fare you well, your suit is cold.'
Cold, indeed, and labour lost.
Then farewell, heat, and welcome, frost.   75
Portia, adieu. I have too grieved a heart
To take a tedious leave. Thus losers part.

Exit Morocco with his train

Portia   A gentle riddance. Draw the curtains, go.
Let all of his complexion choose me so.

Exeunt

Salarino and Solanio report that Shylock has discovered that his daughter Jessica has run away, taking his money and jewels with her. Shylock and the Duke of Venice have tried to search Bassanio's ship, but it has sailed for Belmont. Antonio has confirmed that Jessica and Lorenzo were not on board.

Salarino, Lady and Solanio, 2011

Activity 1: Exploring different points of view

a. In pairs, read aloud lines 1–27.

b. In lines 1–27, Salarino and Solanio report events. Think about what Shylock and the Duke might have been experiencing during those events. Bear in mind that the Duke is Christian and it is his job to rule Venice.

c. Now decide who will play Shylock and the Duke. The person playing Shylock tells the story of what has happened from his point of view, as if he is relating the events to a friend. The other person asks questions to help them understand what has happened.

d. Now the person playing the Duke retells the events, as if to a friend. Again the 'friend' asks questions.

e. Discuss any disagreements you might have had with each other's interpretation.

f. Write a **monologue** in modern English for your character, based on your retelling of the events reported in lines 1–27.

g. Read your monologue to your partner, who can offer advice on any improvements that could be made.

Glossary

8 **gondola** traditional canal boat used in Venice

10 **certified** assured

19 **double ducats** gold coins worth twice the value of single ducats

20 **stones** jewels

25 **look** be sure

25 **keep his day** repay his debt on time

28 **reasoned with** talked with

Key term

Monologue a long speech in which a character expresses their thoughts. Other characters may be present

Act 2 | Scene 8

Enter Salarino and Solanio

Salarino Why, man, I saw Bassanio under sail.
With him is Gratiano gone along,
And in their ship I am sure Lorenzo is not.

Solanio The villain Jew with outcries raised the Duke,
Who went with him to search Bassanio's ship.   5

Salarino He comes too late, the ship was under sail;
But there the Duke was given to understand
That in a gondola were seen together
Lorenzo and his amorous Jessica.
Besides, Antonio certified the Duke   10
They were not with Bassanio in his ship.

Solanio I never heard a passion so confused,
So strange, outrageous, and so variable
As the dog Jew did utter in the streets:
'My daughter! O my ducats! O my daughter!   15
Fled with a Christian! O my Christian ducats!
Justice, the law, my ducats, and my daughter!
A sealèd bag, two sealèd bags of ducats,
Of double ducats, stolen from me by my daughter!
And jewels, two stones, two rich and precious stones,   20
Stolen by my daughter! Justice! Find the girl,
She hath the stones upon her, and the ducats!'

Salarino Why, all the boys in Venice follow him,
Crying, 'His stones, his daughter, and his ducats!'

Solanio Let good Antonio look he keep his day,   25
Or he shall pay for this.

Salarino Marry, well remembered.
I reasoned with a Frenchman yesterday,

Salarino has heard of a Venetian merchant ship wrecked in the English Channel. Solanio advises him to tell Antonio. Salarino describes the moment of parting between Antonio and Bassanio when Bassanio left for Belmont. They go to try to cheer Antonio up.

At the time

Using the context section on page 213, find out about the risks for merchant ships, to help you with the activity on this page.

Activity 2: Exploring the themes of love and friendship

a. In pairs, read aloud lines 36–50, swapping readers at each punctuation mark.
b. Paraphrase lines 36–50 and line 51.
c. Decide who will play Antonio and Bassanio. Create a freeze-frame of them parting, as it is described in lines 36–50. Use information you found for the 'At the time' task to help you.
d. Still in your freeze-frame, take it in turns to speak aloud your character's thoughts, again using information you found for the 'At the time' task to help you.
e. What have you learned about Antonio and Bassanio from tasks a–d? How do you think they feel about each other, and why?
f. Imagining you are the character you have been playing, write a letter to the other character. Include your character's hopes, fears, feelings and advice in your letter.

Glossary

29 **narrow seas** the English Channel
31 **fraught** laden with goods
40 **Slubber not** do not hurry or be careless
41 **stay... time** wait for exactly the right moment
45 **ostents** displays
46 **become you** be appropriate
49 **affection** emotion
49 **wondrous sensible** amazingly felt
51 **he... him** i.e. Bassanio is all he lives for
53 **quicken... heaviness** lighten his chosen sadness

Who told me, in the narrow seas that part
The French and English there miscarried   30
A vessel of our country richly fraught.
I thought upon Antonio when he told me,
And wished in silence that it were not his.

Solanio   You were best to tell Antonio what you hear.
Yet do not suddenly, for it may grieve him.   35

Salarino   A kinder gentleman treads not the earth.
I saw Bassanio and Antonio part.
Bassanio told him he would make some speed
Of his return. He answered, 'Do not so,
Slubber not business for my sake, Bassanio,   40
But stay the very riping of the time.
And for the Jew's bond which he hath of me,
Let it not enter in your mind of love.
Be merry, and employ your chiefest thoughts
To courtship and such fair ostents of love   45
As shall conveniently become you there.'
And even there, his eye being big with tears,
Turning his face, he put his hand behind him,
And with affection wondrous sensible
He wrung Bassanio's hand, and so they parted.   50

Solanio   I think he only loves the world for him.
I pray thee let us go and find him out,
And quicken his embracèd heaviness
With some delight or other.

Salarino   Do we so.

Exeunt

The Prince of Arragon comes to Belmont to see if he can choose the casket that contains Portia's portrait and claim her as his bride.

The Prince of Arragon and Portia, 2015

Did you know?

The meaning of the words in a play depend on the way the actors speak them. Tone, **emphasis**, volume and pace are as important as the dictionary definition of the words in terms of conveying meaning.

Activity 1: Exploring the theme of deceptive appearances — the Prince of Arragon

a. In pairs, decide who will play Portia and the Prince of Arragon. Read aloud lines 4–19.

b. Read the lines again, as if Portia is telling Arragon the facts and Arragon is weighing up the consequences should he fail the challenge.

c. Read the lines again, this time as if Portia is warning Arragon of the consequences and Arragon is proving his love for Portia.

d. Discuss how tone, emphasis, volume and pace help to bring out different interpretations of the characters and what they are thinking.

e. Write down what your character would be thinking during lines 4–19, and why. Include what your character would be thinking about deceptive appearances. Share your work with your partner.

Glossary

s.d. **Servitor** servant
2 **Arragon** region of Spain
3 **election** choice
6 **solemnized** performed
9 **enjoined** bound
17 **hazard** gamble
18 **addressed** prepared
25 **show** appearance
26 **fond** foolish
27 **martlet** house martin, swift (types of birds)

Key term

Emphasis stress given to words when speaking

Act 2 | Scene 9

Enter Nerissa and a Servitor

Nerissa Quick, quick, I pray thee draw the curtain straight.
The Prince of Arragon hath ta'en his oath,
And comes to his election presently.

Enter the Prince of Arragon, his train and Portia

Portia Behold, there stand the caskets, noble Prince.
If you choose that wherein I am contained,   5
Straight shall our nuptial rites be solemnized.
But if thou fail, without more speech, my lord,
You must be gone from hence immediately.

Arragon I am enjoined by oath to observe three things:
First, never to unfold to anyone   10
Which casket 'twas I chose; next, if I fail
Of the right casket, never in my life
To woo a maid in way of marriage. Lastly,
If I do fail in fortune of my choice,
Immediately to leave you and be gone.   15

Portia To these injunctions everyone doth swear
That comes to hazard for my worthless self.

Arragon And so have I addressed me. Fortune now
To my heart's hope. Gold, silver, and base lead.
'Who chooseth me must give and hazard all he hath.'   20
You shall look fairer, ere I give or hazard.
What says the golden chest? Ha, let me see.
'Who chooseth me shall gain what many men desire.'
What many men desire. That 'many' may be meant
By the fool multitude that choose by show,   25
Not learning more than the fond eye doth teach,
Which pries not to th'interior, but like the martlet

The Prince of Arragon chooses the silver casket.

Portia and the Prince of Arragon, 2011

Activity 2: Exploring the theme of value – the Prince of Arragon

a. In pairs, read aloud lines 30–51, swapping readers at each punctuation mark.
b. Using the glossary, paraphrase lines 30–51.
c. One of you read aloud lines 30–51, while the other one listens and whispers aloud any words connected to status or social value.
d. Pick out all the words you whispered.
e. Discuss how Portia might feel as she listens to the Prince of Arragon.
f. Write a paragraph that explains how the imagery the Prince of Arragon uses in lines 30–51 helps us to understand:
   i. what he is thinking and feeling
   ii. how what he says develops the theme of value.

Glossary

28 **Builds... wall** builds its nest in an exposed place
29 **force and road** power and path
37 **cozen** cheat
40 **estates... offices** status; ranks; official jobs
43 **cover... bare** keep their hats on instead of taking them off out of respect for their superiors
45–46 **How... honour?** How many poor born but honourable people would be picked out to rule?
47 **chaff** the part of the wheat plant that is thrown away
48 **new-varnished** polished
50 **assume desert** claim worth
53 **blinking** goggle-eyed
54 **schedule** written scroll
60–61 **To... natures** i.e. Portia cannot judge because she has (unwittingly) offended

Builds in the weather on the outward wall,
Even in the force and road of casualty.
I will not choose what many men desire,   30
Because I will not jump with common spirits
And rank me with the barbarous multitudes.
Why, then to thee, thou silver treasure-house.
Tell me once more what title thou dost bear.
'Who chooseth me shall get as much as he deserves.'   35
And well said too, for who shall go about
To cozen fortune and be honourable
Without the stamp of merit? Let none presume
To wear an undeservèd dignity.
O that estates, degrees and offices   40
Were not derived corruptly, and that clear honour
Were purchased by the merit of the wearer.
How many then should cover that stand bare?
How many be commanded that command?
How much low peasantry would then be gleaned   45
From the true seed of honour? And how much honour
Picked from the chaff and ruin of the times
To be new-varnished. Well, but to my choice.
'Who chooseth me shall get as much as he deserves.'
I will assume desert. Give me a key for this,   50
And instantly unlock my fortunes here.

Arragon unlocks the silver casket

Portia   Too long a pause for that which you find there.

Arragon   What's here? The portrait of a blinking idiot
Presenting me a schedule. I will read it.
How much unlike art thou to Portia.   55
How much unlike my hopes and my deservings.
'Who chooseth me shall have as much as he deserves.'
Did I deserve no more than a fool's head?
Is that my prize? Are my deserts no better?

Portia   To offend and judge are distinct offices   60
And of opposèd natures.

The Prince of Arragon reads the scroll he finds inside the silver casket, says he is a fool and leaves. A messenger brings the news that a young Venetian has come to woo Portia, bearing gifts.

Portia and Nerissa, 2011

Key term
Dialogue a discussion between two or more people

Activity 3: Exploring Portia's attitude to the Prince of Arragon

a. In pairs, decide who will play Portia and Nerissa. Read aloud lines 78–83.

b. Read the lines again, but this time whisper as if the characters are talking about something secret and do not want to be overheard.

c. Stand about five steps apart and read the lines again, loudly.

d. Discuss how these different ways of reading the lines change your understanding of lines 78–83.

e. Discuss:
   i. what the characters are feeling
   ii. Portia's attitude to Prince Arragon.

f. Look at the photo on this page. Who do you think the characters are addressing their lines to during lines 78–83?

g. Summarise lines 78–83 into three or four lines of **dialogue** in modern English that Portia and Nerissa might speak at the moment shown in the photo.

Glossary

62 **The... this** The silver that this casket is made of was purified in fire seven times

65 **shadows** illusions

67 **iwis** for sure

70 **I... head** i.e. whoever you marry, you will always be a fool

77 **wroth** anger; grief

79 **deliberate** calculating

81 **heresy** mistaken belief

88 **sensible regreets** tangible greetings

89 **commends** compliments

89 **courteous breath** polite speech

Arragon   What is here?
          [He reads] 'The fire seven times tried this;
          Seven times tried that judgement is
          That did never choose amiss.
          Some there be that shadows kiss,   65
          Such have but a shadow's bliss.
          There be fools alive, iwis,
          Silvered o'er, and so was this.
          Take what wife you will to bed,
          I will ever be your head.   70
          So begone, you are sped.'
     Still more fool I shall appear
     By the time I linger here.
     With one fool's head I came to woo,
     But I go away with two.   75
     Sweet, adieu. I'll keep my oath,
     Patiently to bear my wroth.

          Exeunt Arragon and train

Portia   Thus hath the candle singed the moth.
          O these deliberate fools! When they do choose,
          They have the wisdom by their wit to lose.   80

Nerissa   The ancient saying is no heresy:
          Hanging and wiving goes by destiny.

Portia   Come, draw the curtain, Nerissa.

          Enter Messenger

Messenger Where is my lady?

Portia   Here, what would my lord?

Messenger Madam, there is alighted at your gate   85
          A young Venetian, one that comes before
          To signify th'approaching of his lord,
          From whom he bringeth sensible regreets,
          To wit, besides commends and courteous breath,
          Gifts of rich value. Yet I have not seen   90

Portia and Nerissa go to find out who the new suitor from Venice is. Nerissa hopes it is Bassanio.

Portia and Nerissa, 2015

At the time

Using the context section on page 219, find out who Cupid was and how Shakespeare's audience would have imagined him, to help you with the activity on this page.

Activity 4: Exploring Portia's state of mind

a. Look back over Act 2 Scene 9. Discuss what state of mind Portia is in at the end of Act 2 Scene 9, and why.

b. Using information you found for the 'At the time' task, imagine you are Portia.

   i. Write down one word that describes what Portia is feeling.

   ii. Write down one sentence in modern English that Portia would like to say and who she would like to say it to. It could be any other character in the play, God or anyone you choose, for example, 'I wonder who this new suitor is?' to Nerissa.

   iii. Write down one thing in modern English that Portia would like to do, for example, 'I wish I could rip up my father's will'.

c. In groups, compare your sentences and combine them in order to create a monologue that Portia might speak.

Glossary

91 **likely** good looking; promising
93 **costly** bountiful
93 **at hand** near
94 **fore-spurrer** one who rides ahead
96 **anon** now
97 **high-day** holiday
99 **Cupid** god of desire
99 **post** messenger
99 **mannerly** politely

So likely an ambassador of love.
A day in April never came so sweet
To show how costly summer was at hand,
As this fore-spurrer comes before his lord.

Portia   No more, I pray thee. I am half afeard   95
Thou wilt say anon he is some kin to thee,
Thou spend'st such high-day wit in praising him.
Come, come, Nerissa, for I long to see
Quick Cupid's post that comes so mannerly.

Nerissa   Bassanio, Lord Love, if thy will it be!   100

Exeunt

Exploring Act 2

Portia, 2011

Activity 1: Designing Act 2

Look back over Act 2. Use the page summaries to help you remember what happens.

a. Where does the action of Act 2 take place? Imagine you are the designer of a production of *The Merchant of Venice*. Write down all the locations for the action that you would need. For example, you might include the place in which the caskets are kept.

b. What are the essential props for Act 2? Write a list of props you would need. For example, you might include the ducats and jewels that Jessica steals from her father's house in Act 2 Scene 6.

c. What would you say was the overall mood of Act 2? What colours might suit that mood?

d. Write notes on, draw or make a model of your stage design for Act 2.

Jessica and Shylock, 2011

Activity 2: Exploring characters in Act 2

a. In groups, choose one of the following characters:
   - Lancelot
   - Jessica
   - Gratiano
   - Portia

   Look back over Act 2 and make a note of your chosen character's actions. You may wish to use a diagram such as a flow chart or spider diagram.

b. Discuss the ways in which your chosen character has been changed by the events of Act 2. Add these to your diagram.

c. Share your diagram with another group. Add any other useful ideas to your diagram.

d. Predict what you think will happen to your chosen character in Act 3.

Solanio and Salarino report that Antonio has lost one of his ships at sea. Shylock comes in and lets them know that he knows they were involved in helping his daughter Jessica to run away.

Solanio, Servant and Salarino, 2011

Glossary

2 **it... unchecked** an undisputed rumour persists

3 **lading** cargo

3 **the narrow seas** the English Channel

3 **Goodwins** a major shipping hazard in the middle of the Channel

4 **flat** sandbank

7 **Knapped ginger** proverbially, nibbled ginger

9 **prolixity** tedious explanations

10 **plain... talk** good, honest communication

16 **betimes** quickly

22 **withal** with

23 **fledged** ready to fly the nest

24 **complexion** disposition

Activity 1: Exploring the function of minor characters

a. In pairs, decide who will play Solanio and Salarino. Read aloud lines 1–15.

b. Read aloud lines 1–15 again, as if the characters are casually gossiping.

c. Read again, this time as if the characters are urgently sharing what they have heard.

d. Discuss how Antonio's friends feel as they speak lines 1–15.

e. Look at the photo on this page, which shows Solanio and Salarino at this moment in the play. Write down five words inspired by the photo that could be used to describe the **atmosphere** and mood of this moment in this production.

f. Write a paragraph that explains why you think Shakespeare chose to include lines 1–15 in the play, including what the dramatic function of Solanio and Salarino is at this moment.

Key terms

Atmosphere the mood created by **staging** choices

Staging the process of selecting, adapting and developing the stage space in which a play will be performed

Act 3 | Scene 1

Enter Solanio and Salarino

Solanio   Now, what news on the Rialto?

Salarino   Why, yet it lives there unchecked that Antonio hath a ship of rich
lading wrecked on the narrow seas, the Goodwins I think they call
the place, a very dangerous flat and fatal, where the carcasses of
many a tall ship lie buried, as they say, if my gossip's report be an   5
honest woman of her word.

Solanio   I would she were as lying a gossip in that as ever knapped ginger
or made her neighbours believe she wept for the death of a third
husband. But it is true, without any slips of prolixity or crossing
the plain highway of talk, that the good Antonio, the honest   10
Antonio – O that I had a title good enough to keep his name
company!

Salarino   Come, the full stop.

Solanio   Ha, what sayest thou? Why, the end is he hath lost a ship.

Salarino   I would it might prove the end of his losses.   15

Solanio   Let me say 'amen' betimes lest the devil cross my prayer, for here
he comes in the likeness of a Jew.

Enter Shylock

How now, Shylock! What news among the merchants?

Shylock   You knew, none so well, none so well as you, of my daughter's
flight.   20

Salarino   That's certain. I, for my part, knew the tailor that made the wings
she flew withal.

Solanio   And Shylock, for his own part, knew the bird was fledged, and
then it is the complexion of them all to leave the dam.

Shylock complains about his daughter. When Salarino mentions the rumour that Antonio has lost a ship, Shylock condemns the way that Antonio and his Christian friends have treated him, and swears revenge.

Shylock, 2015

Glossary

26 **the devil** i.e. Shylock
28 **carrion** rotting flesh
28 **these years** i.e. your old age
32 **Rhenish** fine white wine
34 **match** deal
36 **mart** market (i.e. the Rialto)
36 **look to** remember
38 **courtesy** charity
42 **hindered... million** prevented me from earning half a million ducats
46 **dimensions** parts of the body
54 **sufferance** endurance
56 **I... instruction** I will improve on what you have taught me

Activity 2: Exploring pronouns and the theme of prejudice

a. In pairs, decide who will play Shylock and Salarino. Read aloud lines 29–40, hitting your script each time the word 'flesh' is used.

b. Discuss the reasons why you think the word 'flesh' is repeated during this exchange.

c. Now take turns to read aloud Shylock's speech from lines 41–56, swapping reader after each punctuation mark.

d. Read lines 41–56 again, swapping reader as before, but this time emphasise the **pronouns** by pointing to yourself when you say 'me', 'my', 'I' or 'us', pointing to your partner when you say 'you', and pointing to an imaginary other at your side when you say 'he'. How does this change your understanding of the speech?

e. Imagine you are Shylock. Write a letter to the Duke of Venice, explaining how you feel in lines 29–56. Include ideas about flesh, blood and prejudice in your letter.

Key terms

Pronoun a word (such as *I, he, she, you, it, we* or *they*) that is used instead of a noun

Themes the main ideas explored in a piece of literature, e.g. the themes of love and friendship, fathers and daughters, justice and mercy, prejudice, deceptive appearances and value might be considered key themes of *The Merchant of Venice*

Shylock	She is damned for it.	25
Salarino	That's certain, if the devil may be her judge.	
Shylock	My own flesh and blood to rebel!	
Solanio	Out upon it, old carrion, rebels it at these years?	
Shylock	I say my daughter is my flesh and blood.	

Salarino There is more difference between thy flesh and hers than between   30
jet and ivory, more between your bloods than there is between red
wine and Rhenish. But tell us, do you hear whether Antonio have
had any loss at sea or no?

Shylock There I have another bad match, a bankrupt, a prodigal, who
dare scarce show his head on the Rialto, a beggar that was used   35
to come so smug upon the mart. Let him look to his bond. He was
wont to call me usurer. Let him look to his bond. He was wont to
lend money for a Christian courtesy. Let him look to his bond.

Salarino Why, I am sure if he forfeit, thou wilt not take his flesh. What's
that good for?   40

Shylock To bait fish withal. If it will feed nothing else, it will feed my
revenge. He hath disgraced me, and hindered me half a million,
laughed at my losses, mocked at my gains, scorned my nation,
thwarted my bargains, cooled my friends, heated mine enemies,
and what's the reason? I am a Jew. Hath not a Jew eyes? Hath not   45
a Jew hands, organs, dimensions, senses, affections, passions? Fed
with the same food, hurt with the same weapons, subject to the
same diseases, healed by the same means, warmed and cooled by
the same winter and summer, as a Christian is? If you prick us,
do we not bleed? If you tickle us, do we not laugh? If you poison   50
us, do we not die? And if you wrong us, shall we not revenge? If
we are like you in the rest, we will resemble you in that. If a Jew
wrong a Christian, what is his humility? Revenge. If a Christian
wrong a Jew, what should his sufferance be by Christian example?
Why, revenge. The villainy you teach me I will execute, and it   55
shall go hard but I will better the instruction.

Enter a Servant from Antonio

A servant comes to take Solanio and Salarino to Antonio's house. Tubal brings news from Genoa that Jessica cannot be found. Shylock mourns the loss of his money and jewels, and wishes his daughter dead. Tubal confirms the rumour that Antonio has lost his ship.

Activity 3: Exploring Shylock's state of mind and the theme of value

a. Read aloud lines 65–75. As you read, stand up on the first full stop, sit down on the next one, and then continue standing up or sitting down every time you come to a full stop or question mark. When you come to a comma, stamp your foot.

b. With a partner, discuss what impact the use of punctuation has in this speech. The punctuation is an indicator of a character moving from one thought to another. What state of mind would you say Shylock is in? How do you think he is feeling during this speech? Why might that be?

c. Write a short report explaining what you think Shylock's state of mind is at this stage in the play. Use evidence from lines 65–75 and ideas about value in your writing.

Shylock, 2011

Glossary

60 **matched** found to equal these two
66 **Frankfurt** where there was an annual jewellery fair
66 **The curse** God's curse on the Jews
69 **hearsed** in her coffin
73 **satisfaction** compensation
74 **lights o'** settles on
74 **o'my** of my
78 **argosy** merchant ship
78 **cast away** shipwrecked
83 **fourscore** eighty

Servant	Gentlemen, my master Antonio is at his house and desires to speak with you both.
Salarino	We have been up and down to seek him.

Enter Tubal

Solanio	Here comes another of the tribe. A third cannot be matched, unless the devil himself turn Jew.	60

Exeunt Solanio, Salarino and Servant

Shylock	How now, Tubal, what news from Genoa? Hast thou found my daughter?	
Tubal	I often came where I did hear of her, but cannot find her.	
Shylock	Why, there, there, there, there. A diamond gone, cost me two thousand ducats in Frankfurt. The curse never fell upon our nation till now, I never felt it till now. Two thousand ducats in that, and other precious, precious jewels. I would my daughter were dead at my foot, and the jewels in her ear. Would she were hearsed at my foot, and the ducats in her coffin. No news of them, why, so? And I know not how much is spent in the search. Why, thou loss upon loss. The thief gone with so much, and so much to find the thief, and no satisfaction, no revenge, nor no ill luck stirring but what lights o'my shoulders, no sighs but o'my breathing, no tears but o'my shedding.	65 70 75
Tubal	Yes, other men have ill luck too. Antonio, as I heard in Genoa—	
Shylock	What, what, what? Ill luck, ill luck?	
Tubal	Hath an argosy cast away, coming from Tripolis.	
Shylock	I thank God, I thank God. Is it true, is it true?	
Tubal	I spoke with some of the sailors that escaped the wreck.	80
Shylock	I thank thee, good Tubal, good news, good news. Ha, ha, heard in Genoa.	
Tubal	Your daughter spent in Genoa, as I heard, one night fourscore ducats.	

Tubal reveals that Antonio has received a ring from Jessica in exchange for a monkey. The ring was given to Shylock by his wife before they were married. Shylock sends Tubal to hire an officer to arrest Antonio and then asks Tubal to meet him at the synagogue.

Tubal and Shylock, 2008

Activity 4: Exploring status

a. In pairs, decide who will play Shylock and Tubal. Read aloud lines 85–97.

b. Using information you found for the 'At the time' task, discuss what the turquoise ring might mean to Shylock.

c. Read the lines again, this time with Tubal sitting on a chair while Shylock moves around him.

d. Read the lines again. This time, swap over so that Shylock sits on the chair while Tubal moves.

e. What have you discovered about the relationship between Shylock and Tubal in tasks a–d?

f. Look at the photo on this page. How does it reflect the relationship you found between Shylock and Tubal?

g. Look back over Act 3 Scene 1. List the characters that appear in the scene and those that are referred to.

h. Status is made up of a combination of social and personal power. List the characters in order of highest status to lowest status.

i. Write a paragraph explaining which character in Act 3 Scene 1 has the highest status, in your opinion. Give reasons for your answer.

At the time

Using the context section on page 220, find out what the giving of a ring meant, to help you with the activity on this page.

Glossary

86 **at a sitting** in one go

87 **divers** several

88 **break** bankrupt

94 **Leah** We don't know who this character is – this is the only time she is mentioned. Some critics think she must be Shylock's wife

96 **undone** ruined

97 **fee** hire

98 **bespeak** engage

98 **before** i.e. before the bond is due

99 **what merchandise** whatever business deals

100 **will** want

Shylock	Thou stick'st a dagger in me. I shall never see my gold again. Fourscore ducats at a sitting, fourscore ducats.	85
Tubal	There came divers of Antonio's creditors in my company to Venice that swear he cannot choose but break.	
Shylock	I am very glad of it. I'll plague him, I'll torture him. I am glad of it.	90
Tubal	One of them showed me a ring that he had of your daughter for a monkey.	
Shylock	Out upon her! Thou torturest me, Tubal. It was my turquoise, I had it of Leah when I was a bachelor. I would not have given it for a wilderness of monkeys.	95
Tubal	But Antonio is certainly undone.	
Shylock	Nay, that's true, that's very true. Go, Tubal, fee me an officer, bespeak him a fortnight before. I will have the heart of him if he forfeit, for were he out of Venice I can make what merchandise I will. Go, Tubal, and meet me at our synagogue. Go, good Tubal, at our synagogue, Tubal.	100

Exeunt

In Belmont, Portia asks Bassanio to wait a while before he takes the casket challenge because she wants him to make the right choice. Bassanio wants to choose.

Portia and Bassanio, 2015

At the time

Using the context section on page 222, find out how society expected daughters to behave towards their fathers, to help you with the activity on this page.

Activity 1: Exploring the theme of fathers and daughters — Portia and Bassiano

a. In groups, read aloud lines 1–24, swapping readers at the end of each line.

b. Read the lines again, but this time listen carefully and, before you read your lines, repeat out loud the last few words the previous speaker said. Use those words to help you deliver your own lines more convincingly.

c. What do you think Portia's fear is? Make a **freeze-frame** that shows Portia's fear.

d. Choose a line from lines 1–24 as a title for your freeze-frame.

e. Using information you found for the 'At the time' task, discuss why you think Portia does not teach Bassanio how to choose the right casket. What prevents her?

f. Imagine you are Portia. In modern English, write an anonymous blog explaining your fears, based on lines 1–24.

Glossary

1 **tarry** wait
3 **forbear** have patience
6 **Hate... quality** hatred would not give advice in this way
8 **a... thought** a modest young woman cannot speak what she thinks
11 **am forsworn** have broken the vow made to my father
14 **Beshrew** curse
15 **o'erlooked** bewitched
19 **bars** obstacles
22 **piece** prolong
24 **stay** prevent
24 **election** choice
25 **rack** instrument of torture on which people were stretched
28 **mistrust** doubt; worry

Key term

Freeze-frame a physical, still image created by people to represent an object, place, person or feeling

Act 3 | Scene 2

Enter Bassanio, Portia, Gratiano, Nerissa, and all their trains

Portia I pray you tarry. Pause a day or two
Before you hazard, for in choosing wrong
I lose your company. Therefore forbear awhile.
There's something tells me, but it is not love,
I would not lose you, and you know yourself,   5
Hate counsels not in such a quality.
But lest you should not understand me well,
And yet a maiden hath no tongue but thought,
I would detain you here some month or two
Before you venture for me. I could teach you   10
How to choose right, but then I am forsworn.
So will I never be. So may you miss me.
But if you do, you'll make me wish a sin,
That I had been forsworn. Beshrew your eyes,
They have o'erlooked me and divided me.   15
One half of me is yours, the other half yours,
Mine own, I would say. But if mine, then yours,
And so all yours. O, these naughty times
Puts bars between the owners and their rights.
And so, though yours, not yours. Prove it so,   20
Let fortune go to hell for it, not I.
I speak too long, but 'tis to piece the time,
To eke it and to draw it out in length,
To stay you from election.

Bassanio   Let me choose,
For as I am, I live upon the rack.   25

Portia Upon the rack, Bassanio? Then confess
What treason there is mingled with your love.

Bassanio None but that ugly treason of mistrust,

Portia calls for music whilst Bassanio makes his choice.

Portia, 2011

Key terms

Gesture a movement, often using the hands or head, to express a feeling or idea

Tone as in 'tone of voice'; expressing an attitude through how you say something

Emphasis stress given to words when speaking

Pace the speed at which someone speaks

Extended metaphor describing something by comparing it to something else over several lines

Glossary

30 **amity** friendship

38 **deliverance** release, (i.e. from death)

44 **swan-like end** Swans were thought to sing as they died

49 **flourish** trumpet fanfare

51 **dulcet** sweet

55 **Alcides** Hercules, who rescued Hesione from a sea monster

56 **howling** grieving

58 **Dardanian wives** Trojan women (Dardanus was the founder of Troy)

59 **blearèd visages** tear-stained faces

60 **issue** outcome

61 **Live thou** if you live

62 **fray** assault

Activity 2: Exploring metaphor

a. In pairs, decide who will play Portia and Bassanio. Read aloud lines 24–39.

b. Read the lines aloud again, this time tapping your script every time one of the characters says a key word to do with torture, treason or confession.

c. Create **gestures** for those key words. For example, for 'rack' in line 25, you could wring your hands as if they are stretching and torturing.

d. Read the lines aloud again, adding your gestures and using **tone**, **emphasis** and **pace** to make your understanding of the meaning of the words clear.

e. Discuss how the characters feel as they speak lines 24–39. How effective is the **extended metaphor** they use here?

f. Write a paragraph suggesting why Shakespeare uses the extended metaphor in lines 24–39, and evaluating how effective the metaphor is.

12

	Which makes me fear the enjoying of my love.	
	There may as well be amity and life	30
	'Tween snow and fire, as treason and my love.	
Portia	Ay, but I fear you speak upon the rack,	
	Where men enforcèd do speak anything.	
Bassanio	Promise me life, and I'll confess the truth.	
Portia	Well then, confess and live.	
Bassanio	Confess and love	35
	Had been the very sum of my confession.	
	O happy torment, when my torturer	
	Doth teach me answers for deliverance.	
	But let me to my fortune and the caskets.	
Portia	Away, then. I am locked in one of them.	40
	If you do love me, you will find me out.	
	Nerissa and the rest, stand all aloof.	
	Let music sound while he doth make his choice,	
	Then if he lose, he makes a swan-like end,	
	Fading in music. That the comparison	45
	May stand more proper, my eye shall be the stream	
	And watery death-bed for him. He may win,	
	And what is music then? Then music is	
	Even as the flourish when true subjects bow	
	To a new-crownèd monarch. Such it is,	50
	As are those dulcet sounds in break of day,	
	That creep into the dreaming bridegroom's ear,	
	And summon him to marriage. Now he goes,	
	With no less presence but with much more love	
	Than young Alcides when he did redeem	55
	The virgin tribute paid by howling Troy	
	To the sea-monster. I stand for sacrifice;	
	The rest aloof are the Dardanian wives,	
	With blearèd visages come forth to view	
	The issue of th'exploit. Go, Hercules.	60
	Live thou, I live. With much, much more dismay	
	I view the fight than thou that mak'st the fray.	

A song is sung whilst Bassanio considers his choice. Bassanio says that, in all walks of life, often things that look good on the surface are bad underneath.

Bassanio, 2011

Activity 3: Exploring the theme of deceptive appearances – Bassanio

a. In groups, read aloud lines 73–96, swapping readers at each punctuation mark.

b. Bassanio gives examples of how things that superficially look good in law, religion, bravery and beauty are often bad underneath.

c. Choose law, religion, bravery or beauty. Pick out the lines that relate to that area of life, from lines 73–96.

d. Create a freeze-frame that shows what is being described in your chosen lines.

e. Bring your freeze-frame to life by speaking your chosen lines. As you speak, show what is being described by Bassanio.

f. Share your work with another group.

g. Write a paragraph explaining how lines 73–96 contribute to the theme of deceptive appearances.

Here music. A song the whilst Bassanio comments on the
caskets to himself

SONG Tell me where is fancy bred,
   Or in the heart, or in the head?
   How begot, how nourishèd?   65
   Reply, reply.
   It is engendered in the eyes,
   With gazing fed, and fancy dies
   In the cradle where it lies.
   Let us all ring fancy's knell.   70
   I'll begin it: Ding, dong, bell.

All Ding, dong, bell.

Bassanio So may the outward shows be least themselves,
The world is still deceived with ornament.
In law, what plea so tainted and corrupt,   75
But being seasoned with a gracious voice,
Obscures the show of evil? In religion,
What damnèd error, but some sober brow
Will bless it and approve it with a text,
Hiding the grossness with fair ornament?   80
There is no vice so simple but assumes
Some mark of virtue on his outward parts.
How many cowards whose hearts are all as false
As stairs of sand wear yet upon their chins
The beards of Hercules and frowning Mars,   85
Who, inward searched, have livers white as milk?
And these assume but valour's excrement
To render them redoubted. Look on beauty,
And you shall see 'tis purchased by the weight,
Which therein works a miracle in nature,   90
Making them lightest that wear most of it.
So are those crispèd snaky golden locks
Which makes such wanton gambols with the wind
Upon supposèd fairness, often known
To be the dowry of a second head,   95
The skull that bred them in the sepulchre.

Bassanio chooses the leaden casket and finds Portia's portrait inside.

At the time

Using the context section on page 219, find out about the conventions of courtly love.

Glossary

97 **guilèd** treacherous

99 **Indian** i.e. dark skinned. The Elizabethans thought only light skin was beautiful

102 **Hard... Midas** Everything Midas touched turned to gold, including food

103 **drudge** servant

109 **rash-embraced** recklessly adopted

112 **measure** moderation

114 **surfeit** overindulge

115 **counterfeit** image

115 **demigod** i.e. the artist

116 **Move... eyes** Are the portrait's eyes moving?

117 **balls... mine** my eyeballs

118 **severed** parted

126 **unfurnished** unfinished; unpartnered

127 **substance** subject (i.e. Portia)

Did you know?

An actor at the RSC will go through the text carefully in order to learn more about the character they are playing. They often write a list of what their character says about themselves and other people, and what other people say about them.

Activity 4: Exploring Portia's portrait

a. In groups, read aloud lines 115–126, swapping readers at each punctuation mark.

b. Write a list of all the ways in which Bassanio describes Portia's features in the portrait.

c. Each choose a different description from your list and **paraphrase** it, using the glossary.

d. Create an individual **statue** that shows your chosen description of Portia's portrait.

e. Share your work with the rest of your group.

f. Read aloud lines 115–126 again, swapping readers at each punctuation mark, as if Bassanio is genuinely impressed by the portrait.

g. Read the lines aloud again, swapping readers at each punctuation mark, this time as if Bassanio is describing the portrait in an over the top way in order to impress Portia.

h. Using information you found for the 'At the time' task, write a paragraph explaining how Bassanio describes Portia's portrait in lines 115–126 and why you think he does so.

Key terms

Paraphrase put a line or section of text into your own words

Statue like a freeze-frame but usually of a single character

Thus ornament is but the guilèd shore
To a most dangerous sea, the beauteous scarf
Veiling an Indian beauty; in a word,
The seeming truth which cunning times put on   100
To entrap the wisest. Therefore, then, thou gaudy gold,
Hard food for Midas, I will none of thee.
Nor none of thee, thou pale and common drudge
'Tween man and man. But thou, thou meagre lead,
Which rather threaten'st than dost promise aught,   105
Thy paleness moves me more than eloquence,
And here choose I. Joy be the consequence.

Portia   [Aside] How all the other passions fleet to air,
As doubtful thoughts and rash-embraced despair
And shuddering fear and green-eyed jealousy.   110
O love, be moderate, allay thy ecstasy,
In measure rain thy joy, scant this excess.
I feel too much thy blessing. Make it less,
For fear I surfeit.

Bassanio opens the leaden casket

Bassanio   What find I here?
Fair Portia's counterfeit. What demigod   115
Hath come so near creation? Move these eyes?
Or whether, riding on the balls of mine,
Seem they in motion? Here are severed lips
Parted with sugar breath; so sweet a bar
Should sunder such sweet friends. Here in her hairs   120
The painter plays the spider, and hath woven
A golden mesh t'entrap the hearts of men
Faster than gnats in cobwebs. But her eyes,
How could he see to do them? Having made one,
Methinks it should have power to steal both his   125
And leave itself unfurnished. Yet look how far
The substance of my praise doth wrong this shadow

Bassanio reads the scroll from inside the leaden casket, which invites him to claim Portia as his wife. Portia says that she is young and unpractised in the ways of the world, and she wishes she had more to offer Bassanio.

Activity 5: Exploring costume design and the theme of deceptive appearances

a. In pairs, read aloud lines 149–163, swapping readers at the end of each line.

b. Read the lines again, but this time listen carefully to your partner and, before you read your lines, repeat out loud the last few words your partner spoke. Use those words to help you deliver your own line more convincingly.

c. Look at the photo on this page and at what Bassanio says in lines 88–96. Discuss the following:

  i. What do you think Portia is trying to achieve during lines 149–165?

  ii. What do you think she is feeling? Why?

  iii. Why do you think Portia took off her blonde wig at this moment in this production.

  iv. How might this idea affect what the audience thinks about Portia in this scene?

  v. How might this idea help to develop the theme of appearances being deceptive?

Portia, 2011

Glossary

128 **shadow** image
130 **continent** summation
132 **Chance as fair** choose as fortunately
140 **note** i.e. as directed by the scroll
155 **account** estimate; financial reckoning
156 **livings** possessions
157 **sum** essence; financial amount
158 **gross** overall

In underprizing it, so far this shadow
Doth limp behind the substance. Here's the scroll,
The continent and summary of my fortune.   130
[He reads] 'You that choose not by the view
    Chance as fair and choose as true.
    Since this fortune falls to you,
    Be content and seek no new.
    If you be well pleased with this   135
    And hold your fortune for your bliss,
    Turn you where your lady is
    And claim her with a loving kiss.'
A gentle scroll. Fair lady, by your leave,
I come by note to give and to receive.   140
Like one of two contending in a prize
That thinks he hath done well in people's eyes,
Hearing applause and universal shout,
Giddy in spirit, still gazing in a doubt
Whether those peals of praise be his or no,   145
So, thrice-fair lady, stand I, even so,
As doubtful whether what I see be true,
Until confirmed, signed, ratified by you.

Portia   You see me, Lord Bassanio, where I stand,
Such as I am. Though for myself alone   150
I would not be ambitious in my wish,
To wish myself much better, yet for you
I would be trebled twenty times myself,
A thousand times more fair, ten thousand times
More rich, that only to stand high in your account,   155
I might in virtues, beauties, livings, friends,
Exceed account. But the full sum of me
Is sum of nothing, which to term in gross
Is an unlessoned girl, unschooled, unpractisèd,
Happy in this, she is not yet so old   160
But she may learn. Happier than this,
She is not bred so dull but she can learn;
Happiest of all is that her gentle spirit
Commits itself to yours to be directed,

Portia gives Bassanio a ring as a symbol that she gives herself and everything she owns to him. Bassanio swears he will not take off the ring until he dies. Gratiano asks if there can be a double wedding because he and Nerissa are in love.

Bassanio, Portia and Nerissa, 2015

At the time

Using the context section on page 222, find out whether women were legally allowed to own property. Find out what the Elizabethans thought about a witnessed betrothal.

Key term

Motivation a person's reason for doing something

Activity 6: Exploring motivation

a. In pairs, decide who will play Portia and Bassanio. Read aloud lines 166–185.
b. Look at the photo on this page and think about the information you found for the 'At the time' task.
c. Create a freeze-frame of the characters at this moment in the play.
d. Still in your freeze-frame, take turns to speak aloud your thoughts, from the point of view of your character.
e. Share your work with another pair.
f. What have you learned about Portia and Bassanio from tasks a–e?
g. Look back over Act 3 Scene 2. Choose either Bassanio or Portia, and write a paragraph analysing their **motivation** during lines 166–185, using quotations from Act 3 Scene 2.

Glossary

167 **But now** a moment ago
173 **presage** indicate
174 **vantage** opportunity
174 **exclaim on** accuse
176 **my blood speaks** I am blushing
178 **oration** public speech
181 **blent** blended
182 **wild** wilderness
182 **save** except
191 **none from** no joy away from
192–193 **solemnize The bargain** formalise the agreement (i.e. get married)
195 **so** if

As from her lord, her governor, her king.   165
Myself, and what is mine, to you and yours
Is now converted. But now I was the lord
Of this fair mansion, master of my servants,
Queen o'er myself, and even now, but now,
This house, these servants and this same myself   170
Are yours, my lord. I give them with this ring,
Which when you part from, lose or give away,
Let it presage the ruin of your love
And be my vantage to exclaim on you.

Bassanio   Madam, you have bereft me of all words.   175
Only my blood speaks to you in my veins,
And there is such confusion in my powers,
As after some oration fairly spoke
By a belovèd prince there doth appear
Among the buzzing pleasèd multitude,   180
Where every something being blent together
Turns to a wild of nothing save of joy
Expressed and not expressed. But when this ring
Parts from this finger, then parts life from hence.
O then be bold to say Bassanio's dead.   185

Nerissa   My lord and lady, it is now our time,
That have stood by and seen our wishes prosper,
To cry good joy, good joy, my lord and lady!

Gratiano   My Lord Bassanio and my gentle lady,
I wish you all the joy that you can wish,   190
For I am sure you can wish none from me.
And when your honours mean to solemnize
The bargain of your faith, I do beseech you,
Even at that time I may be married too.

Bassanio   With all my heart, so thou canst get a wife.   195

Gratiano   I thank your lordship, you have got me one.
My eyes, my lord, can look as swift as yours.
You saw the mistress, I beheld the maid.
You loved, I loved; for intermission

It is agreed that Gratiano and Nerissa will be married at the same time as Bassanio and Portia. Lorenzo, Jessica and a messenger called Salerio arrive from Venice. Bassanio welcomes them to Belmont.

Nerissa and Gratiano, 2008

At the time

Using the context section on page 216, find out what the traditional features of a comedy were.

Activity 7: Exploring listening

a. In groups, decide who will play Gratiano, Nerissa, Portia and Bassanio. Read aloud lines 206–215.
b. Read the lines again, but this time listen carefully and, before you read your lines, repeat out loud a significant phrase the previous speaker said. Use that phrase to help you deliver your own lines more convincingly.
c. Using information you found for the 'At the time' task, discuss:
    i. whether or not Gratiano and Nerissa's relationship is a surprise to Portia and Bassanio
    ii. what difference it makes to Act 3 Scene 2 that Gratiano announces that he and Nerissa want to get married.
d. Write down what you would be thinking during lines 206–215, and why, from the point of view of the character that you played.

Glossary

201 **stood** depended
204 **swearing… dry** declaring love till the roof of my mouth was parched
209 **so… withal** if you are happy with it
210 **faith** intentions
213 **We'll… ducats** We'll bet a thousand ducats on which couple has the first son
214 **stake down** the money for the bet on the table
216 **infidel** faithless one
219 **youth** newness
219 **new interest** newly acquired authority
221 **very** true
227 **past… nay** would not let me refuse

No more pertains to me, my lord, than you.   200
Your fortune stood upon the caskets there,
And so did mine too, as the matter falls.
For wooing here until I sweat again,
And swearing till my very roof was dry
With oaths of love, at last, if promise last,   205
I got a promise of this fair one here
To have her love, provided that your fortune
Achieved her mistress.

Portia   Is this true, Nerissa?

Nerissa   Madam, it is so, so you stand pleased withal.

Bassanio   And do you, Gratiano, mean good faith?   210

Gratiano   Yes, faith, my lord.

Bassanio   Our feast shall be much honoured in your marriage.

Gratiano   We'll play with them the first boy for a thousand ducats.

Nerissa   What, and stake down?

Gratiano   No, we shall ne'er win at that sport and stake down.   215
But who comes here? Lorenzo and his infidel?
What, and my old Venetian friend Salerio?

Enter Lorenzo, Jessica and Salerio, a messenger from Venice

Bassanio   Lorenzo and Salerio, welcome hither,
If that the youth of my new interest here
Have power to bid you welcome. By your leave,   220
I bid my very friends and countrymen,
Sweet Portia, welcome.

Portia   So do I, my lord.
They are entirely welcome.

Lorenzo   I thank your honour. For my part, my lord,
My purpose was not to have seen you here,   225
But meeting with Salerio by the way,
He did entreat me, past all saying nay,
To come with him along.

Salerio gives Bassanio a letter from Antonio, which he reads. Portia notices Bassanio's reaction to the letter and he confirms that the letter contains bad news. Bassanio confesses to Portia that he is in debt.

Bassanio, 2008

Activity 8: Exploring character — Bassanio

a. Read lines 249–258. Discuss the bad news that the letter contains.

b. Look at the photo on this page. What does it suggest about Bassanio's state of mind at the end of Act 3 Scene 2?

c. Imagine you are Bassanio.
   i. Write down one word that describes what Bassanio is feeling.
   ii. Write down one sentence in modern English that Bassanio would like to say and who he would like to say it to. It could be any other character in the play, God or anyone you choose, for example, 'Shylock, how can you be so cruel?'
   iii. Write down one thing in modern English that Bassanio would like to do, for example, 'I wish I could turn back time.'

d. In groups, compare your sentences and combine them in order to create a **monologue** that Bassanio might speak.

Salerio	I did, my lord, And I have reason for it. [Giving letter] Signor Antonio Commends him to you.	
Bassanio	Ere I ope his letter, I pray you tell me how my good friend doth.	230
Salerio	Not sick, my lord, unless it be in mind, Nor well, unless in mind. His letter there Will show you his estate.	

Bassanio opens the letter

Gratiano	Nerissa, cheer yond stranger, bid her welcome. Your hand, Salerio. What's the news from Venice? How doth that royal merchant, good Antonio? I know he will be glad of our success. We are the Jasons, we have won the fleece.	235
Salerio	I would you had won the fleece that he hath lost.	240
Portia	There are some shrewd contents in yond same paper, That steals the colour from Bassanio's cheek. Some dear friend dead, else nothing in the world Could turn so much the constitution Of any constant man. What, worse and worse? With leave, Bassanio, I am half yourself, And I must freely have the half of anything That this same paper brings you.	245
Bassanio	O sweet Portia, Here are a few of the unpleasantest words That ever blotted paper. Gentle lady, When I did first impart my love to you, I freely told you all the wealth I had Ran in my veins: I was a gentleman; And then I told you true. And yet, dear lady, Rating myself at nothing, you shall see How much I was a braggart. When I told you My state was nothing, I should then have told you That I was worse than nothing; for indeed	250 255

Salerio confirms that all Antonio's ventures have failed and describes how Shylock is insisting that Antonio pays the forfeit, despite the Duke of Venice trying to persuade him to be lenient. Jessica says her father would rather have a pound of Antonio's flesh than money.

Bassanio, Jessica, Portia, Lorenzo, Gratiano and Salerio, 2015

Activity 9: Exploring the theme of prejudice – Jessica and Portia

a. In groups, decide who will play Salerio, Jessica, Portia and Bassanio.

b. The person playing Salerio should read aloud lines 269–281 twice:
   i. as if Salerio cannot believe how Shylock is behaving
   ii. as if Salerio is angry about how Shylock is behaving.

c. Discuss which version felt most appropriate and why.

d. The person playing Jessica should read aloud lines 282–288 twice:
   i. as if Jessica is accusing her father and Portia is pleased with her
   ii. as if Jessica is realising that her father wants revenge, and Portia is dismissive of her.

e. Discuss which version felt most appropriate for Jessica and Portia, and why.

f. Write a paragraph that explains who you think is being prejudiced at this moment, and why.

Glossary

260 **Engaged** pledged
260 **mere** total
261 **To… means** to get the money I needed
265 **hit** success
271 **discharge** pay
276 **impeach** call into question
278 **magnificoes** fine gentlemen
279 **port** dignity; social standing
288 **hard with** badly for
292 **courtesies** good services

I have engaged myself to a dear friend,
Engaged my friend to his mere enemy   260
To feed my means. Here is a letter, lady,
The paper as the body of my friend,
And every word in it a gaping wound
Issuing life-blood. But is it true, Salerio?
Hath all his ventures failed? What, not one hit?   265
From Tripolis, from Mexico and England,
From Lisbon, Barbary and India?
And not one vessel 'scape the dreadful touch
Of merchant-marring rocks?

Salerio   Not one, my lord.
Besides, it should appear that if he had   270
The present money to discharge the Jew,
He would not take it. Never did I know
A creature that did bear the shape of man
So keen and greedy to confound a man.
He plies the Duke at morning and at night,   275
And doth impeach the freedom of the state
If they deny him justice. Twenty merchants,
The Duke himself, and the magnificoes
Of greatest port have all persuaded with him,
But none can drive him from the envious plea   280
Of forfeiture, of justice and his bond.

Jessica   When I was with him I have heard him swear
To Tubal and to Chus, his countrymen,
That he would rather have Antonio's flesh
Than twenty times the value of the sum   285
That he did owe him. And I know, my lord,
If law, authority and power deny not,
It will go hard with poor Antonio.

Portia   Is it your dear friend that is thus in trouble?

Bassanio   The dearest friend to me, the kindest man,   290
The best-conditioned and unwearied spirit
In doing courtesies, and one in whom

Portia clarifies the sum that Antonio owes Shylock. She suggests Bassanio marries her and then goes to Venice to pay the debt with gold she will give him. Bassanio reads the letter, in which Antonio asks his friend to come to see him before he dies. In return, Antonio will cancel all debts between them.

Did you know?

To help actors feel connected to the words they speak, they sometimes use objects, such as the chairs in the activity on this page, to represent physically the feelings behind the words.

Bassanio and Portia, 2008

Activity 10: Exploring dialogue

a. In pairs, decide who will play Portia and Bassanio. Read aloud lines 295–323.

b. Place two chairs facing each other and stand behind them. Read lines 295–323 again, this time moving your chairs in relation to each other as the relationship between the characters develops. For example, if you think that your character is challenging the other person, you might put your chair down directly in front of them. Try to follow your instincts rather than planning how you will move the chair next.

c. Discuss the following:

   i. How would you describe the relationship between Portia and Bassanio during lines 295–323?

   ii. Who would you say was in control, and why?

   iii. How does this link to ideas of men and women you examined at the end of Act 1? How are Portia and Bassanio following – or not – stereotypical ideas about how men and women of their time behaved?

d. Look at the photo on this page. How would you describe the relationship between Portia and Bassanio at this moment? How far does this agree with the relationship you discovered through tasks a–c?

Glossary

293 **ancient Roman honour** i.e. loyalty to friends and country

297 **deface** obliterate

309 **shall hence** go from here

314 **estate** condition; status

317 **use your pleasure** do what you wish

319 **Dispatch** settle

323 **'twixt us twain** between us two

Key term

Dialogue a discussion between two or more people

The ancient Roman honour more appears
Than any that draws breath in Italy.

Portia   What sum owes he the Jew? 295

Bassanio   For me three thousand ducats.

Portia   What, no more?
Pay him six thousand and deface the bond.
Double six thousand and then treble that,
Before a friend of this description
Shall lose a hair through Bassanio's fault. 300
First go with me to church and call me wife,
And then away to Venice to your friend;
For never shall you lie by Portia's side
With an unquiet soul. You shall have gold
To pay the petty debt twenty times over. 305
When it is paid, bring your true friend along.
My maid Nerissa and myself meantime
Will live as maids and widows. Come, away,
For you shall hence upon your wedding day.
Bid your friends welcome, show a merry cheer; 310
Since you are dear bought, I will love you dear.
But let me hear the letter of your friend.

Bassanio   [Reads] 'Sweet Bassanio, my ships have all miscarried, my
creditors grow cruel, my estate is very low, my bond to the Jew is
forfeit; and since in paying it, it is impossible I should live, all debts 315
are cleared between you and I if I might see you at my death.
Notwithstanding, use your pleasure. If your love do not persuade
you to come, let not my letter.'

Portia   O love! Dispatch all business, and be gone.

Bassanio   Since I have your good leave to go away, 320
I will make haste; but till I come again,
No bed shall e'er be guilty of my stay,
No rest be interposer 'twixt us twain.

Exeunt

In Venice, Shylock instructs the jailer to guard Antonio. Antonio tries to persuade Shylock to listen to him, but Shylock will not hear him, and leaves. Solanio sympathises with Antonio, but Antonio is sure that Shylock hates him because he has helped others pay their debts to the moneylender.

Antonio and Shylock, 2015

Activity 1: Exploring subtext and the theme of prejudice

a. In pairs, decide who will play Antonio and Shylock. Read aloud lines 3–17.

b. Read lines 3–17 again, with the person playing Antonio listening quietly and politely to Shylock.

c. Read lines 3–17 again. This time the person playing Antonio can interrupt Shylock with comments and questions at any time, and say what Antonio is thinking when he hears Shylock's words. The person playing Shylock should try not to be put off by these interruptions.

d. Discuss:
  i. what difference the interruptions made to Shylock
  ii. what difference the interruptions made to Antonio
  iii. the most powerful words used by your character
  iv. what your character would be thinking and feeling during lines 3–17.

e. Write a paragraph that explains the subtext of lines 3–17, and why Shakespeare gives Shylock most of the lines to speak. Use the idea of prejudice in your writing. Include the words from lines 3–17 that you think are the most powerful, explaining why.

Did you know?

In rehearsals, actors try different exercises, like the one on this page, to help them understand how the characters feel. When an actor knows how their character feels, they can use the language to express those feelings to the audience.

Glossary

1 **look to him** guard him
2 **gratis** without interest
9 **naughty** wicked
9 **fond** foolish
10 **abroad** out of the jail; outside
19 **kept** lived
20 **bootless** pointless
22 **delivered** rescued
22 **forfeitures** penalties for breach of contract

Key term

Subtext the underlying meaning in the script

Act 3 | Scene 3

Enter Shylock, Solanio, Antonio and the Jailer

Shylock   Jailer, look to him. Tell not me of mercy.
This is the fool that lends out money gratis.
Jailer, look to him.

Antonio   Hear me yet, good Shylock.

Shylock   I'll have my bond. Speak not against my bond.
I have sworn an oath that I will have my bond.   5
Thou calledst me dog before thou hadst a cause,
But since I am a dog, beware my fangs.
The Duke shall grant me justice. I do wonder,
Thou naughty Jailer, that thou art so fond
To come abroad with him at his request.   10

Antonio   I pray thee hear me speak.

Shylock   I'll have my bond. I will not hear thee speak.
I'll have my bond and therefore speak no more.
I'll not be made a soft and dull-eyed fool,
To shake the head, relent, and sigh, and yield   15
To Christian intercessors. Follow not.
I'll have no speaking, I will have my bond.

Exit Shylock

Solanio   It is the most impenetrable cur
That ever kept with men.

Antonio   Let him alone.
I'll follow him no more with bootless prayers.   20
He seeks my life. His reason well I know:
I oft delivered from his forfeitures
Many that have at times made moan to me,
Therefore he hates me.

131

Antonio tells his friend Solanio that the Venetian legal system applies to all, including foreigners. He prays that Bassanio will arrive in time to see him pay his debt of a pound of flesh.

Antonio, 2011

At the time

Using the context section on page 213, find out about the Venetian legal system, to help you with the activity on this page.

Activity 2: Exploring the themes of justice and mercy

a. Read lines 26–36, then paraphrase them.

b. Who does Antonio say justice applies to in the state of Venice?

c. Using information you found for the 'At the time' task, consider how Shakespeare's audience would have understood what Antonio says in lines 26–36.

d. Look at the photo on this page, which shows this moment in performance. The **director** of this production chose a contemporary American prison uniform as Antonio's costume and had Antonio deliver lines 26–36 into a microphone so that his voice filled the theatre.

  i. In what ways do you think these production choices might have affected the audience's understanding of the themes of justice and mercy in the play?

  ii. Discuss whether or not you agree with the director's choices, and why.

Glossary

25 **grant** allow
25 **hold** stand
27 **commodity** privileges
27 **strangers** foreigners (including Jewish people)
31 **Consisteth** consists
32 **bated me** diminished me

Key term

Director the person who enables the practical and creative interpretation of a dramatic script, and ultimately brings together everybody's ideas in a way that engages the audience with the play

Solanio   I am sure the Duke
                        Will never grant this forfeiture to hold.   25

Antonio   The Duke cannot deny the course of law,
                        For the commodity that strangers have
                        With us in Venice, if it be denied,
                        Will much impeach the justice of the state,
                        Since that the trade and profit of the city   30
                        Consisteth of all nations. Therefore go.
                        These griefs and losses have so bated me,
                        That I shall hardly spare a pound of flesh
                        Tomorrow to my bloody creditor.
                        Well, Jailer, on. Pray God, Bassanio come   35
                        To see me pay his debt, and then I care not.

Exeunt

In Belmont, Lorenzo praises Portia for letting Bassanio go to Venice to help Antonio. Portia reasons that Antonio, being so close to Bassanio, must be worth helping. She asks Lorenzo to manage her household while she and Nerissa go to live in a monastery until their husbands' return.

Portia, Jessica and Lorenzo, 2015

Activity 1: Exploring the themes of love and friendship – Portia

a. In groups, read aloud lines 10–21, swapping readers at the end of each line.
b. Read the lines again, but this time listen carefully and, before you read your lines, repeat out loud the last few words the previous speaker said. Use those words to help you deliver your own lines more convincingly.
c. Paraphrase lines 10–21.
d. Make a freeze-frame that shows the relationship between Portia, Bassanio and Antonio at this point in the play.
e. Share your work with another group, explaining choices you have made.
f. Discuss why you think Portia is willing to help Antonio.
g. Imagine you are Portia. Write a summary of what she says in lines 10–21 in the style of a diary entry or blog, including the ideas of love and friendship.

Glossary

2 **conceit** understanding
3 **godlike amity** divine friendship
9 **bounty** generosity
14 **like** similar
15 **lineaments** appearances
19 **bestowed** spent
20 **semblance** likeness
20 **my soul** i.e. my soulmate, Bassanio
25 **husbandry** domestic administration

Act 3 | Scene 4

Enter Portia, Nerissa, Lorenzo, Jessica and Balthasar (a man of Portia's)

Lorenzo   Madam, although I speak it in your presence,
You have a noble and a true conceit
Of godlike amity, which appears most strongly
In bearing thus the absence of your lord.
But if you knew to whom you show this honour,   5
How true a gentleman you send relief,
How dear a lover of my lord your husband,
I know you would be prouder of the work
Than customary bounty can enforce you.

Portia   I never did repent for doing good,   10
Nor shall not now; for in companions
That do converse and waste the time together,
Whose souls do bear an equal yoke of love,
There must be needs a like proportion
Of lineaments, of manners and of spirit,   15
Which makes me think that this Antonio,
Being the bosom lover of my lord,
Must needs be like my lord. If it be so,
How little is the cost I have bestowed
In purchasing the semblance of my soul   20
From out the state of hellish cruelty.
This comes too near the praising of myself,
Therefore no more of it. Hear other things:
Lorenzo, I commit into your hands
The husbandry and manage of my house   25
Until my lord's return. For mine own part,
I have toward heaven breathed a secret vow
To live in prayer and contemplation,
Only attended by Nerissa here,
Until her husband and my lord's return.   30

It is agreed that Lorenzo and Jessica will look after Belmont for Portia. Portia sends Balthasar with a letter to her cousin Doctor Bellario in Padua. She instructs Balthasar to collect some papers and clothes from Bellario, and then meet her and Nerissa in Venice.

Portia, Jessica and Lorenzo, 2008

Activity 2: Exploring the action

a. In groups, read aloud lines 45–55, swapping readers at each punctuation mark.

b. Choose three moments you think tell the story of Portia's plan in lines 45–55. Create three freeze-frames showing Portia, Nerissa, Balthasar and Doctor Bellario, as you think they would be at your chosen moments.

c. Discuss what you think the 'notes and garments' are that Doctor Bellario will give Balthasar.

d. Write a paragraph explaining Portia's plan in lines 45–55. In your explanation, predict what the 'notes and garments' are.

Glossary

33 **deny** refuse
33 **imposition** command
37 **people** servants
52 **imagined speed** as fast as you can imagine
53 **traject** crossing place
54 **trades** i.e. crosses
57 **work** a plan
59 **think of us** expect us

There is a monastery two miles off
And there we will abide. I do desire you
Not to deny this imposition,
The which my love and some necessity
Now lays upon you.

Lorenzo   Madam, with all my heart,   35
I shall obey you in all fair commands.

Portia My people do already know my mind
And will acknowledge you and Jessica
In place of Lord Bassanio and myself.
So fare you well till we shall meet again.   40

Lorenzo Fair thoughts and happy hours attend on you.

Jessica I wish your ladyship all heart's content.

Portia I thank you for your wish, and am well pleased
To wish it back on you. Fare you well Jessica.

Exeunt Jessica and Lorenzo

Now, Balthasar,   45
As I have ever found thee honest-true,
So let me find thee still. Take this same letter,
And use thou all the endeavour of a man
In speed to Padua. See thou render this
Into my cousin's hand, Doctor Bellario,   50
And look what notes and garments he doth give thee,
Bring them, I pray thee with imagined speed
Unto the traject, to the common ferry
Which trades to Venice. Waste no time in words,
But get thee gone. I shall be there before thee.   55

Balthasar Madam, I go with all convenient speed.

Exit Balthasar

Portia Come on, Nerissa, I have work in hand
That you yet know not of. We'll see our husbands
Before they think of us.

Portia explains to Nerissa that they will disguise themselves as men. There is a coach and horses waiting to take them on a journey, and Portia says she will explain her whole plan to Nerissa while they are travelling.

At the time

Using the context section on page 222, remind yourself how society expected women to behave, to help you with the activity on this page.

Glossary

60 **habit** clothing
61 **accomplishèd** equipped
62 **that we lack** i.e. male genitals
63 **accoutred** dressed
64 **prettier** smarter
66–67 **between... voice** i.e. as if an adolescent with his voice breaking
67 **mincing** dainty
68 **frays** fights
69 **quaint** elaborate
72 **do withal** help it
77 **raw** crude
77 **bragging Jacks** boastful fellows
80 **lewd interpreter** someone with a dirty mind
81 **device** plan
82 **stays** waits
84 **measure** cover; journey

Activity 3: Exploring imagery

a. In pairs, read aloud lines 60–78, swapping readers at each punctuation mark.
b. Read the lines again, this time hitting your script every time you say a word that describes men or male behaviour.
c. Decide which you think are the most important words in lines 60–78. Choose at least four words.
d. Agree gestures that could go with each of the key words you have chosen. Use gestures that help you to express exactly what the character means. Look at the photo on this page for inspiration.
e. Now read the lines again, adding the gestures.
f. Work through the rest of the speech in the same way.
g. The **imagery** a character uses can give us an idea of what is on their mind. Imagine you have the opportunity to interview Portia for a newspaper article called 'Playing men at their own game'. Write a list of interview questions to find out what Portia hopes to achieve, based on the imagery she uses in lines 60–78.

Key term

Imagery visually descriptive language

Nerissa	Shall they see us?
Portia	They shall, Nerissa, but in such a habit, 60
	That they shall think we are accomplishèd
	With that we lack. I'll hold thee any wager,
	When we are both accoutred like young men,
	I'll prove the prettier fellow of the two,
	And wear my dagger with the braver grace, 65
	And speak between the change of man and boy
	With a reed voice, and turn two mincing steps
	Into a manly stride, and speak of frays
	Like a fine bragging youth, and tell quaint lies,
	How honourable ladies sought my love, 70
	Which I denying, they fell sick and died.
	I could not do withal. Then I'll repent,
	And wish for all that, that I had not killed them.
	And twenty of these puny lies I'll tell,
	That men shall swear I have discontinued school 75
	Above a twelvemonth. I have within my mind
	A thousand raw tricks of these bragging Jacks,
	Which I will practise.
Nerissa	Why, shall we turn to men?
Portia	Fie, what a question's that,
	If thou wert near a lewd interpreter? 80
	But come, I'll tell thee all my whole device
	When I am in my coach, which stays for us
	At the park gate; and therefore haste away,
	For we must measure twenty miles today.

Exeunt

In Belmont, Lancelot Gobbo tells Jessica that she is damned because she was born Jewish. Lorenzo comes in and Jessica tells her husband what Lancelot has been saying.

Jessica and Lancelot Gobbo, 2015

Activity 1: Exploring the theme of fathers and daughters – Lancelot and Jessica

a. In pairs, decide who will play Lancelot and Jessica. Read aloud lines 1–19.

b. Stand a few steps apart. To help you understand more about the characters, the relationships between them and their motives, read lines 1–19 again. This time, as you speak and listen, you should keep choosing between the following movements:
   • Take a step towards another character.
   • Take a step away from another character.
   • Turn towards another character.
   • Turn away from another character.
   • Stand still.
   Try to make instinctive choices rather than planning what to do.

c. Using information you found for the 'At the time' task, discuss what effect Lancelot's words have on Jessica.

d. Write a summary of what happens in lines 1–19 from Jessica's point of view, using the idea of fathers and daughters and quotations from lines 1–19 to explain what happens. You could style this as a blog or an interview.

Key term

Malapropism mistaken use of a word that sounds like another word but has a very different meaning

Act 3 | Scene 5

Enter Lancelot and Jessica

Lancelot Yes truly, for look you, the sins of the father are to be laid upon
the children, therefore, I promise you, I fear you. I was always
plain with you, and so now I speak my agitation of the matter.
Therefore be of good cheer, for truly I think you are damned.
There is but one hope in it that can do you any good, and that is   5
but a kind of bastard hope neither.

Jessica And what hope is that, I pray thee?

Lancelot Marry, you may partly hope that your father got you not, that
you are not the Jew's daughter.

Jessica That were a kind of bastard hope indeed. So the sins of my   10
mother should be visited upon me.

Lancelot Truly then I fear you are damned both by father and mother.
Thus when I shun Scylla, your father, I fall into Charybdis, your
mother. Well, you are gone both ways.

Jessica I shall be saved by my husband. He hath made me a Christian.   15

Lancelot Truly, the more to blame he. We were Christians enow before,
e'en as many as could well live one by another. This making of
Christians will raise the price of hogs. If we grow all to be pork-
eaters, we shall not shortly have a rasher on the coals for money.

Enter Lorenzo

Jessica I'll tell my husband, Lancelot, what you say. Here he comes.   20

Lorenzo I shall grow jealous of you shortly, Lancelot, if you thus get my
wife into corners.

Jessica Nay, you need not fear us, Lorenzo. Lancelot and I are out. He
tells me flatly there is no mercy for me in heaven because I am
a Jew's daughter. And he says, you are no good member of the   25

Lorenzo accuses Lancelot of getting a Moorish woman pregnant. They engage in a battle of wits. Lorenzo instructs Lancelot to bid the servant to get dinner ready, which Lancelot goes to do. Lorenzo asks Jessica how she is.

Lorenzo and Lancelot Gobbo, 2011

Glossary

29 **getting... belly** making the Moorish woman (probably a servant) pregnant

31 **more than reason** bigger than is reasonable

32 **honest** chaste

37 **all stomachs** appetites

40 **'cover'** lay the table

41 **cover** cover your head with a hat

42 **duty** place (servants were bare-headed in the presence of their superiors)

43 **quarrelling with occasion** finding opportunities to wise-crack

48 **humours** mood

49 **conceits** fancies

50 **discretion** judgement

50 **suited** adapted, matched

53 **A** of

53 **stand... place** have superior positions

54 **Garnished** trimmed

55 **Defy the matter** confuse the meaning

Key term

Banter playful dialogue where the speakers verbally score points off each other

Activity 2: Exploring banter

a. In groups, decide who will play Lorenzo and Lancelot. Read aloud lines 28–49.

b. Using the glossary, paraphrase lines 28–49.

c. Read aloud lines 28–49 again. This time, every time one of the characters feels they have scored a point against the other, they should hit their script with their hand. For example, when Lancelot says 'more than reason' in line 31, he should hit his script.

d. Discuss the following:
   i. Who scores the most points?
   ii. In what ways might Jessica react to what is going on between Lancelot and Lorenzo? Do you think she finds it funny or not?

e. Write a paragraph describing how Lancelot and Lorenzo behave during lines 28–49, and the effect of their banter on Jessica.

commonwealth, for in converting Jews to Christians, you raise the
price of pork.

Lorenzo I shall answer that better to the commonwealth than you can the
getting up of the negro's belly. The Moor is with child by you,
Lancelot!   30

Lancelot It is much that the Moor should be more than reason, but if she be
less than an honest woman, she is indeed more than I took her for.

Lorenzo How every fool can play upon the word. I think the best
grace of wit will shortly turn into silence, and discourse grow
commendable in none only but parrots. Go in, sirrah, bid them   35
prepare for dinner.

Lancelot That is done, sir, they have all stomachs.

Lorenzo Goodly lord, what a wit-snapper are you. Then bid them prepare
dinner.

Lancelot That is done too, sir, only 'cover' is the word.   40

Lorenzo Will you cover then, sir?

Lancelot Not so, sir, neither. I know my duty.

Lorenzo Yet more quarrelling with occasion. Wilt thou show the whole
wealth of thy wit in an instant? I pray thee, understand a plain
man in his plain meaning: go to thy fellows, bid them cover the   45
table, serve in the meat, and we will come in to dinner.

Lancelot For the table, sir, it shall be served in; for the meat, sir, it shall be
covered; for your coming in to dinner, sir, why, let it be as humours
and conceits shall govern.

Exit Lancelot

Lorenzo O dear discretion, how his words are suited.   50
The fool hath planted in his memory
An army of good words, and I do know
A many fools that stand in better place,
Garnished like him, that for a tricksy word
Defy the matter. How cheerest thou, Jessica?   55

Lorenzo asks Jessica what she thinks of Portia. They go in to dinner.

Lorenzo and Jessica, 2015

Activity 3: Exploring one character's opinion of another

a. In pairs, read aloud lines 58–68, swapping readers at the end of each sentence.

b. Paraphrase each of the three sentences that Jessica says about Portia in lines 58–68.

c. Choose one of the sentences from task b.

   i. With one of you as Portia and the other as Jessica, work together to create a statue of Portia as Jessica sees her in your chosen sentence.

   ii. The person playing Jessica reads your chosen sentence whilst Portia brings the statue you have created to life.

d. Share your work with another pair, explaining the choices you made.

e. Write a paragraph that explains Jessica's attitude towards Portia, using quotations from lines 58–68.

	And now, good sweet, say thy opinion,	
	How dost thou like the Lord Bassanio's wife?	
Jessica	Past all expressing. It is very meet	
	The Lord Bassanio live an upright life,	
	For, having such a blessing in his lady,	60
	He finds the joys of heaven here on earth.	
	And if on earth he do not merit it,	
	In reason he should never come to heaven.	
	Why, if two gods should play some heavenly match	
	And on the wager lay two earthly women,	65
	And Portia one, there must be something else	
	Pawned with the other, for the poor rude world	
	Hath not her fellow.	
Lorenzo	Even such a husband	
	Hast thou of me as she is for a wife.	
Jessica	Nay, but ask my opinion too of that.	70
Lorenzo	I will anon. First, let us go to dinner.	
Jessica	Nay, let me praise you while I have a stomach.	
Lorenzo	No, pray thee let it serve for table-talk,	
	Then, howsome'er thou speak'st, 'mong other things	
	I shall digest it.	
Jessica	Well, I'll set you forth.	75

Exeunt

Exploring Act 3

Activity 1: Exploring the events of Act 3

a. In groups, look back through Act 3 and agree on three moments that seem the most important. Looking at the page summaries may help you.

b. Choose one or two lines of text for each of your three moments.

c. Create three freeze-frames, showing each of your moments and include a way of speaking your chosen lines of text aloud in your freeze-frames.

d. Record your freeze-frames by photographing, drawing or describing them. Give each one your chosen line as a title.

e. Explain:
   i. why you feel the three moments you chose are the most important
   ii. why you chose the lines of text for each of your three moments
   iii. how your freeze-frames show your chosen moments and lines effectively.

Did you know?

Modern editions of Shakespeare's plays, like this one, divide the play into five Acts and then into scenes within each Act. The five-act structure is useful for understanding the shape of the action. Usually the end of Act 3 or the beginning of Act 4 is the dramatic climax of the play. In *The Merchant of Venice*, by the end of Act 3, all the characters are focused on the imminent moment when Shylock has the right to collect his debt from Antonio. Act 4 Scene 1 marks the climax of the play.

Portia, 2011

Activity 2: Exploring the development of themes in Act 3

a. In groups, look back over Act 3 and each choose one of the following themes:
- Prejudice
- Deceptive appearances
- Fathers and daughters
- Love and friendship
- Value

b. Trace how ideas about your chosen theme have been developed in Act 3. Discuss your ideas and rank the themes in order of their importance in this Act.

c. As a group, prepare a presentation about your chosen theme.

The Duke and Magnificoes of Venice, Antonio and his friends gather in court for Shylock to collect his debt from Antonio. The Duke calls Shylock into court and tells the moneylender that the court expects him not to go through with taking his pound of flesh.

The Duke of Venice, 2015

Glossary

6 **From** of
6 **dram** small measure
7 **qualify** moderate
8 **stands obdurate** remains resolute
10 **envy's** malice
13 **tyranny** cruelty
18–19 **thou... act** you persist in this show of cruelty until the final moment
21 **strange** unnatural
24 **loose** abandon

Did you know?

The entrance into a scene establishes where it takes place, the relationships and attitudes of the characters, and what the **atmosphere** is. The order in which the characters enter and how they come in helps actors and audience to understand a scene.

Activity 1: Exploring an entrance

a. Go through the list of characters under the first **stage direction** 'Enter' on page 149. Decide who the 'others' at the end of that list might be. You can include whoever you like as long as you have a clear reason why the character would be in court when Shylock collects his debt from Antonio.

b. Put the characters in the order of who you think should enter first, then next, until everyone is assembled. Include Shylock at the end of the list, who enters just before line 16.

c. Write a sentence for each character explaining why you think they should enter at that point in the sequence. Your sentence should include what the character's attitude to the event is, an activity they would be doing as they enter, and an **adjective** to describe their behaviour.

Key terms

Atmosphere the mood created by **staging** choices
Stage direction an instruction in the text of a play, e.g. indicating which characters enter and exit a scene
Adjective a word that describes a noun, e.g. *blue*, *happy*, *big*
Staging the process of selecting, adapting and developing the stage space in which a play will be performed

Act 4 | Scene 1

Enter the Duke, the Magnificoes, Antonio, Bassanio, Gratiano, Salerio and others

Duke What, is Antonio here?

Antonio Ready, so please your grace.

Duke I am sorry for thee. Thou art come to answer
A stony adversary, an inhuman wretch
Uncapable of pity, void and empty   5
From any dram of mercy.

Antonio   I have heard
Your grace hath ta'en great pains to qualify
His rigorous course, but since he stands obdurate
And that no lawful means can carry me
Out of his envy's reach, I do oppose   10
My patience to his fury, and am armed
To suffer with a quietness of spirit
The very tyranny and rage of his.

Duke Go one, and call the Jew into the court.

Salerio He is ready at the door. He comes, my lord.   15

Enter Shylock

Duke Make room, and let him stand before our face.
Shylock, the world thinks, and I think so too,
That thou but lead'st this fashion of thy malice
To the last hour of act, and then 'tis thought
Thou'lt show thy mercy and remorse more strange   20
Than is thy strange apparent cruelty.
And where thou now exact'st the penalty,
Which is a pound of this poor merchant's flesh,
Thou wilt not only loose the forfeiture,

The Duke advises Shylock to forget a portion of the sum Antonio borrowed and show mercy to the merchant who has lost his fortune. Shylock insists on collecting the forfeit of his bond and refuses to give a reason other than that he hates Antonio.

Shylock, 2015

Activity 2: Exploring sentence structure and the theme of justice

a. In pairs, read aloud lines 35–62, swapping at each punctuation mark.

b. Read lines 35–62 again, this time swapping at the end of each sentence, breathing only when there is a full stop or a question mark at the end of a sentence.

c. Now look at how many sentences there are in this speech. Discuss the following:

   i. Where in lines 35–62 was it easy to speak the sentences in one breath? At what point does it get more challenging?

   ii. What **pace** do you have to speak at to read the penultimate sentence all in on one breath?

   iii. What happens to your voice when you try to speak it all in one breath?

   iv. What do you think Shylock is feeling when he speaks this sentence, and why?

d. Write a paragraph explaining the effect of the sentence structure in lines 35–62.

Glossary

26 **Forgive** forgo
26 **moiety** portion
26 **principal** the sum borrowed
29 **Enow** enough
30 **commiseration of** sympathy for
31 **brassy bosoms** hard hearts
32 **stubborn** unfeeling
32 **Turks and Tartars** The Elizabethans considered both to be pitiless
33 **offices... courtesy** gentle and polite behaviours
34 **gentle** pun on 'gentile', a non-Jewish person
36 **Sabbath** Saturday, the holy day of the Jewish week
39 **charter** Venice was an independent city, granted by legal charter
41 **carrion** dead; rotten
46 **baned** poisoned
47 **gaping pig** roasted pig's head with an apple in its mouth
50 **affection** instinct
51 **passion** emotion

But touched with humane gentleness and love, 25
Forgive a moiety of the principal,
Glancing an eye of pity on his losses,
That have of late so huddled on his back,
Enow to press a royal merchant down,
And pluck commiseration of his state 30
From brassy bosoms and rough hearts of flint,
From stubborn Turks and Tartars, never trained
To offices of tender courtesy.
We all expect a gentle answer, Jew.

Shylock I have possessed your grace of what I purpose, 35
And by our holy Sabbath have I sworn
To have the due and forfeit of my bond.
If you deny it, let the danger light
Upon your charter and your city's freedom.
You'll ask me why I rather choose to have 40
A weight of carrion flesh than to receive
Three thousand ducats. I'll not answer that,
But say it is my humour. Is it answered?
What if my house be troubled with a rat
And I be pleased to give ten thousand ducats 45
To have it baned? What, are you answered yet?
Some men there are love not a gaping pig,
Some that are mad if they behold a cat,
And others when the bagpipe sings i'th'nose
Cannot contain their urine; for affection, 50
Mistress of passion, sways it to the mood
Of what it likes or loathes. Now for your answer:
As there is no firm reason to be rendered
Why he cannot abide a gaping pig,
Why he a harmless necessary cat, 55
Why he a woollen bagpipe, but of force
Must yield to such inevitable shame
As to offend, himself being offended;
So can I give no reason, nor I will not,
More than a lodged hate and a certain loathing 60
I bear Antonio, that I follow thus

Bassanio accuses Shylock of cruelty, but Shylock will not be put off. Antonio says that a Jewish heart cannot be softened. Bassanio offers Shylock double the amount of the original loan, but Shylock refuses.

Jailer, Antonio and Jailer, 2011

Activity 3: Exploring the theme of prejudice

a. In pairs, read aloud lines 70–80.

b. Create **gestures** for the key words in each line. For example, for 'I pray you' in line 70, you could position your hands as if praying.

c. Read aloud lines 70–80 again, adding your gestures and using **tone**, **emphasis** and pace to make your understanding of the meaning of the words clear.

d. Discuss the following:

   i. What things does Antonio compare Shylock's harshness to?

   ii. How effective are these comparisons?

   iii. Who do you think Antonio is talking to in lines 70–80? Bassanio? The Duke? Shylock? The whole court? Use the photo on this page if you need inspiration.

   iv. What do you think the reactions of the other characters are to Antonio's speech?

e. Write a paragraph that explains how lines 70–80 contribute to the theme of prejudice.

Glossary

62 **losing suit** unprofitable case

64 **current** flow

70 **think** realise

72 **main flood** sea at high tide

72 **bate** hold

76 **wag** sway

82 **brief... conveniency** as quickly and simply as possible

87 **draw** take

92 **parts** duties

Key terms

Gesture a movement, often using the hands or head, to express a feeling or idea

Tone as in 'tone of voice'; expressing an attitude through how you say something

Emphasis stress given to words when speaking

	A losing suit against him. Are you answered?	
Bassanio	This is no answer, thou unfeeling man,	
	To excuse the current of thy cruelty.	
Shylock	I am not bound to please thee with my answer.	65
Bassanio	Do all men kill the things they do not love?	
Shylock	Hates any man the thing he would not kill?	
Bassanio	Every offence is not a hate at first.	
Shylock	What, wouldst thou have a serpent sting thee twice?	
Antonio	I pray you think you question with the Jew.	70
	You may as well go stand upon the beach	
	And bid the main flood bate his usual height;	
	You may as well use question with the wolf	
	Why he hath made the ewe bleat for the lamb.	
	You may as well forbid the mountain pines	75
	To wag their high tops and to make no noise	
	When they are fretted with the gusts of heaven.	
	You may as well do anything most hard	
	As seek to soften that – than which what's harder?—	
	His Jewish heart. Therefore, I do beseech you	80
	Make no more offers, use no farther means,	
	But with all brief and plain conveniency	
	Let me have judgement and the Jew his will.	
Bassanio	For thy three thousand ducats here is six.	
Shylock	If every ducat in six thousand ducats	85
	Were in six parts and every part a ducat,	
	I would not draw them. I would have my bond.	
Duke	How shalt thou hope for mercy, rendering none?	
Shylock	What judgement shall I dread, doing no wrong?	
	You have among you many a purchased slave,	90
	Which, like your asses and your dogs and mules,	
	You use in abject and in slavish parts	
	Because you bought them. Shall I say to you,	

Shylock argues that, just as the Venetians have bought slaves, he has bought Antonio's flesh. The Duke threatens to dismiss the court unless the lawyer, Doctor Bellario of Padua, comes to resolve the dispute. Nerissa, disguised as a lawyer's clerk, arrives with letters from Bellario. Bassanio urges Antonio to have courage, but Antonio has no hope that he will survive.

Bassanio and Nerissa, 2011

Activity 4: Exploring how private or public a moment is

a. In pairs, decide who will play Bassanio and Antonio. Read aloud lines 111–118.

b. Read the lines again, but this time whisper the lines as if Bassanio and Antonio do not want to be overheard by the other characters. How does this change the moment?

c. Stand five paces apart and read the lines again, this time loudly, as if neither character can control their strong emotions. Look at the photo on this page, which shows this moment in performance.

d. Read the lines again, this time varying the volume of your speech according to how you think lines 111–118 should be played.

e. Discuss what you think the other characters should be doing during lines 111–118.

f. If you were staging this moment, how private or public would you make it? Give reasons for your answer.

Glossary

97 **seasoned… viands** treated to your food

101 **fie** shame

107 **stays without** waits outside

114 **tainted wether** diseased sheep

115 **Meetest** most suitable

121 **whet** sharpen

	'Let them be free, marry them to your heirs?	
	Why sweat they under burdens? Let their beds	95
	Be made as soft as yours and let their palates	
	Be seasoned with such viands?' You will answer,	
	'The slaves are ours.' So do I answer you.	
	The pound of flesh which I demand of him	
	Is dearly bought; 'tis mine and I will have it.	100
	If you deny me, fie upon your law!	
	There is no force in the decrees of Venice.	
	I stand for judgement. Answer, shall I have it?	
Duke	Upon my power I may dismiss this court,	
	Unless Bellario, a learnèd doctor,	105
	Whom I have sent for to determine this,	
	Come here today.	
Salerio	My lord, here stays without	
	A messenger with letters from the doctor,	
	New come from Padua.	
Duke	Bring us the letters. Call the messenger.	110
Bassanio	Good cheer, Antonio! What man, courage yet.	
	The Jew shall have my flesh, blood, bones and all,	
	Ere thou shalt lose for me one drop of blood.	
Antonio	I am a tainted wether of the flock,	
	Meetest for death. The weakest kind of fruit	115
	Drops earliest to the ground and so let me.	
	You cannot better be employed, Bassanio,	
	Than to live still and write mine epitaph.	

Enter Nerissa disguised as a lawyer's clerk

Duke	Came you from Padua, from Bellario?	
Nerissa	From both. My lord Bellario greets your grace.	120

She gives a letter to the Duke

Bassanio	Why dost thou whet thy knife so earnestly?	
Shylock	To cut the forfeiture from that bankrupt there.	

Gratiano accuses Shylock of malicious cruelty. Shylock answers that he is following the law. The Duke reads a letter from Bellario explaining that the lawyer is sick and has sent in his place a young lawyer called Balthasar. Court officials go to bring Balthasar into the court.

Activity 5: Exploring the emotional impact of language

a. Read aloud lines 128–129.

b. Read the lines again, but this time emphasise and exaggerate the vowel sounds in the words.

c. Discuss what strong emotion Gratiano might be expressing with these sounds.

d. Read aloud lines 128–138.

e. Read the lines again, but this time hit your script every time you say a word to do with wolves or their behaviour. Discuss:

  i. why you think Gratiano compares Shylock to a wolf

  ii. how effective the **extended metaphor** is in lines 130–138

  iii. what you think Gratiano is feeling as he speaks lines 128–129.

f. Write a paragraph explaining how Gratiano's use of language in lines 128–138 reveals his emotional state.

Gratiano	Not on thy sole, but on thy soul, harsh Jew,
	Thou mak'st thy knife keen. But no metal can,
	No, not the hangman's axe, bear half the keenness 125
	Of thy sharp envy. Can no prayers pierce thee?
Shylock	No, none that thou hast wit enough to make.
Gratiano	O be thou damned, inexecrable dog,
	And for thy life let justice be accused!
	Thou almost mak'st me waver in my faith 130
	To hold opinion with Pythagoras,
	That souls of animals infuse themselves
	Into the trunks of men. Thy currish spirit
	Governed a wolf who, hanged for human slaughter,
	Even from the gallows did his fell soul fleet, 135
	And whilst thou lay'st in thy unhallowed dam,
	Infused itself in thee, for thy desires
	Are wolvish, bloody, starved and ravenous.
Shylock	Till thou canst rail the seal from off my bond,
	Thou but offend'st thy lungs to speak so loud. 140
	Repair thy wit, good youth, or it will fall
	To endless ruin. I stand here for law.
Duke	This letter from Bellario doth commend
	A young and learnèd doctor to our court.
	Where is he?
Nerissa	He attendeth here hard by 145
	To know your answer, whether you'll admit him.
Duke	With all my heart. Some three or four of you
	Go give him courteous conduct to this place.

Exeunt officials

Meantime the court shall hear Bellario's letter.
[Reads] 'Your grace shall understand that at the receipt of your   150
letter I am very sick, but in the instant that your messenger came,
in loving visitation was with me a young doctor of Rome. His
name is Balthasar. I acquainted him with the cause in controversy

Portia, disguised as Balthasar, a young, male, doctor of law, enters the court. The Duke welcomes Balthasar. Antonio confesses that he has failed to repay the bond, so Portia says Shylock must be merciful.

Did you know?

Actors use the rhythm in Shakespeare's language to help them learn their lines and understand the script. Sometimes there are irregularities in the rhythm, which can indicate a character is disturbed in some way. Sometimes characters share the rhythm, which can be a clue about how urgent their conversation is.

Glossary

154 **turned o'er** read
157 **importunity** urging
159 **reverend** respected
162 **commendation** praise
167 **difference** dispute
174 **in such rule** so properly
175 **impugn** call into question

Key terms

Iambic pentameter the rhythm Shakespeare uses to write his plays. Each line in this rhythm contains approximately ten syllables. 'Iambic' means putting the stress on the second syllable of each beat. 'Pentameter' means five beats with two syllables in each beat

Dialogue a discussion between two or more people

Shared lines lines of iambic pentameter shared between characters. This implies a closeness between them in some way

Activity 6: Exploring Shakespeare's rhythm

a. Read the 'Key terms' and 'Did you know?' boxes.
b. Say out loud: 'and ONE, and TWO, and THREE, and FOUR, and FIVE'.
c. Repeat task b and clap the rhythm as you speak.
d. In groups, read aloud lines 166–178. Try fitting the words to the **iambic pentameter** rhythm.
e. Discuss the following:
   i. Line 172 is one iambic pentameter shared between Portia and Shylock. What effect does that have on their **dialogue**?
   ii. Find other examples of **shared lines** in lines 166–178.
f. Write a paragraph arguing what you think Portia's state of mind is in lines 166–178. Use the rhythmic structure of the lines to explain your argument.

between the Jew and Antonio the merchant. We turned o'er many
books together. He is furnished with my opinion, which bettered   155
with his own learning, the greatness whereof I cannot enough
commend, comes with him, at my importunity, to fill up your
grace's request in my stead. I beseech you, let his lack of years
be no impediment to let him lack a reverend estimation, for I
never knew so young a body with so old a head. I leave him   160
to your gracious acceptance, whose trial shall better publish his
commendation.'

Enter Portia disguised as Balthasar

You hear the learnèd Bellario, what he writes,
And here, I take it, is the doctor come.
Give me your hand. Came you from old Bellario?   165

Portia	I did, my lord.
Duke	You are welcome. Take your place. Are you acquainted with the difference That holds this present question in the court?
Portia	I am informèd throughly of the cause. Which is the merchant here, and which the Jew? 170
Duke	Antonio and old Shylock, both stand forth.
Portia	Is your name Shylock?
Shylock	Shylock is my name.
Portia	Of a strange nature is the suit you follow, Yet in such rule that the Venetian law Cannot impugn you as you do proceed. 175 You stand within his danger, do you not?
Antonio	Ay, so he says.
Portia	Do you confess the bond?
Antonio	I do.
Portia	Then must the Jew be merciful.

Portia argues that Shylock should be merciful, but he still insists that the court follow the law and allow him to collect the pound of flesh. Bassanio offers again to repay the loan twice over and begs Balthasar to bend the law to save Antonio's life.

Bassanio, 2015

Activity 7: Exploring the effect of Portia's speech and the theme of justice

a. In groups, read aloud lines 180–201, swapping readers at each punctuation mark.

b. Using the glossary, **paraphrase** lines 180–201.

c. Decide who will listen, as the 'audience' in court. This person should sit on a chair between two other people, who should be close enough to whisper into their ears. The person on the left should whisper lines 180–201. At the same time, the person on the right should whisper your paraphrase of Portia's speech.

d. Swap roles so that each of you has the opportunity to listen.

e. Discuss:
   i. which words from lines 180–201 stood out to you
   ii. what atmosphere is created by lines 180–201
   iii. how Portia's words develop the theme of justice.

f. Write a review describing how Portia's speech made you feel, as if you have been in the audience in court, watching and listening to this moment.

Glossary

180 **strained** forced
186 **temporal** earthly
187 **attribute** possession; quality
193 **seasons** moderates
204 **discharge** pay
205 **tender** offer
210 **bears down** overwhelms
211 **Wrest** bend

Key term

Paraphrase put a line or section of text into your own words

Shylock	On what compulsion must I? Tell me that.

Portia   The quality of mercy is not strained,   180
It droppeth as the gentle rain from heaven
Upon the place beneath. It is twice blest,
It blesseth him that gives and him that takes.
'Tis mightiest in the mightiest, it becomes
The thronèd monarch better than his crown.   185
His sceptre shows the force of temporal power,
The attribute to awe and majesty,
Wherein doth sit the dread and fear of kings.
But mercy is above this sceptred sway,
It is enthronèd in the hearts of kings,   190
It is an attribute to God himself;
And earthly power doth then show likest God's
When mercy seasons justice. Therefore, Jew,
Though justice be thy plea, consider this,
That in the course of justice, none of us   195
Should see salvation. We do pray for mercy,
And that same prayer doth teach us all to render
The deeds of mercy. I have spoke thus much
To mitigate the justice of thy plea,
Which if thou follow, this strict court of Venice   200
Must needs give sentence 'gainst the merchant there.

Shylock   My deeds upon my head. I crave the law,
The penalty and forfeit of my bond.

Portia   Is he not able to discharge the money?

Bassanio   Yes, here I tender it for him in the court,   205
Yea, twice the sum. If that will not suffice,
I will be bound to pay it ten times o'er
On forfeit of my hands, my head, my heart.
If this will not suffice, it must appear
That malice bears down truth. And I beseech you   210
Wrest once the law to your authority.
To do a great right, do a little wrong,
And curb this cruel devil of his will.

Portia explains that making an exception to the law in this case will set a precedent for future cases and therefore cannot be done. She asks Shylock to be merciful and take the money, but still Shylock refuses. Portia tells Antonio he must prepare to have the pound of flesh cut from his chest.

Shylock and Portia, 2008

Activity 8: Exploring objectives, tactics and the theme of justice – Shylock and Portia

a. In pairs, discuss what Shylock and Portia are each trying to achieve in Act 4 Scene 1. What are their objectives?

b. Decide who will play Shylock and Portia. Sitting on chairs, read aloud lines 214–238. Position your chairs in relation to each other according to what you think is the relationship between the characters at the beginning of this section.

c. Read lines 214–238 again, this time moving your chairs in relation to each other as the relationship between the characters develops. For example, if you think that your character is challenging the other person, you might put your chair directly in front of them. If you think your character is sneakily giving information to the other person, you might move your chair to the side.

d. Discuss:
   i. what **motivates** Portia and Shylock during lines 214–238
   ii. what **tactics** Portia and Shylock are using to achieve their objectives
   iii. how lines 214–238 develop the theme of justice.

Glossary

219 **Daniel** In the Apocrypha, Daniel turns the evidence of old men against themselves to prove a woman who is accused of being unchaste not guilty
223 **thrice** three times
231 **tenure** contract
233 **exposition** introductory explanation
235 **pillar** upstanding support
238 **stay** take a stand

Key terms

Objective what a character wants to get or achieve in a scene
Motivation a person's reason for doing something
Tactics the methods a character uses to get what they want

Portia	It must not be. There is no power in Venice
	Can alter a decree establishèd. 215
	'Twill be recorded for a precedent,
	And many an error by the same example
	Will rush into the state. It cannot be.
Shylock	A Daniel come to judgement, yea, a Daniel!
	O wise young judge, how I do honour thee. 220
Portia	I pray you let me look upon the bond.
Shylock	Here 'tis, most reverend doctor, here it is.
Portia	Shylock, there's thrice thy money offered thee.
Shylock	An oath, an oath, I have an oath in heaven.
	Shall I lay perjury upon my soul? 225
	No, not for Venice.
Portia	Why, this bond is forfeit,
	And lawfully by this the Jew may claim
	A pound of flesh, to be by him cut off
	Nearest the merchant's heart. Be merciful.
	Take thrice thy money. Bid me tear the bond. 230
Shylock	When it is paid according to the tenure.
	It doth appear you are a worthy judge,
	You know the law, your exposition
	Hath been most sound. I charge you by the law,
	Whereof you are a well-deserving pillar, 235
	Proceed to judgement. By my soul I swear,
	There is no power in the tongue of man
	To alter me. I stay here on my bond.
Antonio	Most heartily I do beseech the court
	To give the judgement.
Portia	Why then, thus it is: 240
	You must prepare your bosom for his knife.
Shylock	O noble judge! O excellent young man!
Portia	For the intent and purpose of the law

Portia appeals to Shylock to employ a surgeon to be present, to prevent Antonio from dying. Shylock will not because it is not written in the bond. Portia invites Antonio to speak. He says goodbye to Bassanio.

Bassanio and Antonio, 2011

Activity 9: Exploring the theme of love and friendship – Antonio, Bassanio and Portia

a. In groups, read aloud lines 261–277, swapping readers at each punctuation mark.
b. Look through lines 261–277 again and reduce the speech to just 12 words. These words can come from anywhere in lines 261–277, including next to each other.
c. Create a performance of this moment in the play using only your 12 words, accompanied by actions and gestures. Make sure that your tone of voice and **body language** tell the story of what Antonio is saying.
d. Discuss:
    i. how you think Antonio feels about Bassanio
    ii. how you think Bassanio feels about Antonio
    iii. how you think Portia feels about Antonio.

Glossary

244 **Hath... to** fully supports
251 **balance** scales
253 **on your charge** at your expense
260 **armed** prepared
264 **still her use** usually fate's custom
267 **age** old age
270 **process** legal, manner
271 **me fair** well of me

Key term

Body language how we communicate feelings to each other using our bodies (including facial expressions) rather than words

	Hath full relation to the penalty,	
	Which here appeareth due upon the bond.	245
Shylock	'Tis very true. O wise and upright judge!	
	How much more elder art thou than thy looks.	
Portia	Therefore lay bare your bosom.	
Shylock	Ay, his breast,	
	So says the bond, doth it not, noble judge?	
	'Nearest his heart', those are the very words.	250
Portia	It is so. Are there balance here to weigh	
	The flesh?	
Shylock	I have them ready.	
Portia	Have by some surgeon, Shylock, on your charge,	
	To stop his wounds, lest he should bleed to death.	
Shylock	Is it so nominated in the bond?	255
Portia	It is not so expressed, but what of that?	
	'Twere good you do so much for charity.	
Shylock	I cannot find it, 'tis not in the bond.	
Portia	Come, merchant, have you anything to say?	
Antonio	But little. I am armed and well prepared.	260
	Give me your hand, Bassanio. Fare you well.	
	Grieve not that I am fallen to this for you,	
	For herein Fortune shows herself more kind	
	Than is her custom. It is still her use	
	To let the wretched man outlive his wealth,	265
	To view with hollow eye and wrinkled brow	
	An age of poverty, from which lingering penance	
	Of such misery doth she cut me off.	
	Commend me to your honourable wife.	
	Tell her the process of Antonio's end.	270
	Say how I loved you, speak me fair in death,	
	And when the tale is told, bid her be judge	
	Whether Bassanio had not once a love.	

Bassanio says he would sacrifice his wife and his own life to save Antonio. Gratiano says he too would give up his wife to save his friend. Shylock condemns them. Portia says the law allows and the court awards Shylock a pound of Antonio's flesh. But, as Shylock is about to cut, Portia tells him to wait. The bond does not give Shylock any of Antonio's blood.

Shylock and Antonio, 2011

Jailer, Shylock, Antonio (lying down) and Jailer, 2008

Jailer, Antonio and Shylock, 2015

Activity 10: Exploring a power relationship

a. In pairs, decide who will play Portia and Shylock. Read aloud lines 291–303.

b. Look at the photos on this page, which show this scene in performance. If you were Portia observing Shylock's behaviour, how would you react?

c. Read aloud lines 291–303 again. This time the person playing Portia should start by holding an object such as a pencil case or a bottle of water, and the person playing Shylock must take the object as they speak their own line. Continue taking the object from each other throughout lines 291–303. The person holding the object can make it easy or difficult for the other person to take it.

d. Discuss and note down the moments at which you grabbed the object and how that happened.

e. Make a list of vocabulary to describe Portia and Shylock's behaviour. Use this vocabulary to write a paragraph explaining how Portia and Shylock communicate during lines 291–303.

Glossary

279 **Which** who
283 **deliver** free
290 **else** otherwise
292 **Would** I wish
292 **Barabbas** in the Bible, the thief released by Pontius Pilate instead of Jesus
294 **trifle** waste
295 **thine** yours
301 **Tarry** wait
302 **jot** drop

	Repent not you that you shall lose your friend,	
	And he repents not that he pays your debt.	275
	For if the Jew do cut but deep enough,	
	I'll pay it instantly with all my heart.	
Bassanio	Antonio, I am married to a wife	
	Which is as dear to me as life itself,	
	But life itself, my wife, and all the world,	280
	Are not with me esteemed above thy life.	
	I would lose all, ay, sacrifice them all	
	Here to this devil, to deliver you.	
Portia	Your wife would give you little thanks for that	
	If she were by to hear you make the offer.	285
Gratiano	I have a wife, whom I protest I love,	
	I would she were in heaven, so she could	
	Entreat some power to change this currish Jew.	
Nerissa	'Tis well you offer it behind her back,	
	The wish would make else an unquiet house.	290
Shylock	These be the Christian husbands. I have a daughter;	
	Would any of the stock of Barabbas	
	Had been her husband rather than a Christian.	
	We trifle time. I pray thee pursue sentence.	
Portia	A pound of that same merchant's flesh is thine.	295
	The court awards it, and the law doth give it.	
Shylock	Most rightful judge.	
Portia	And you must cut this flesh from off his breast.	
	The law allows it, and the court awards it.	
Shylock	Most learnèd judge. A sentence; come, prepare!	300
Portia	Tarry a little, there is something else.	
	This bond doth give thee here no jot of blood,	
	The words expressly are 'a pound of flesh'.	
	Then take thy bond, take thou thy pound of flesh,	
	But in the cutting it, if thou dost shed	305

167

Portia explains that if Shylock sheds one drop of Antonio's blood, all his property and wealth will be confiscated by the state. Shylock says he will take three times the original sum in payment and let Antonio go, but Portia says that Shylock must have the justice he has insisted on. She invites Shylock to take his pound of flesh.

Key term

Blocking the movements agreed for staging a scene

Gratiano and Shylock, 2015

Activity 11: Exploring power and movement

a. In groups, decide who will play Portia, Gratiano, Shylock and Bassanio. Read aloud lines 308–333.

b. The people playing Portia, Gratiano and Bassanio stand rooted to the spot. They are not allowed to move. Meanwhile, the person playing Shylock moves wherever they like around the others, experimenting with how they can use their physical presence to intimidate the other characters, without touching them. Read aloud lines 308–333 again, using these rules.

c. Read the lines again, this time with Shylock rooted to the spot and the other characters able to move wherever they like around him.

d. Discuss the following:
   i. Who is challenging who, and when, during this section?
   ii. How could you move to show that?
   iii. Look at the photo on this page and discuss which line you think is being spoken here, and why.

e. Write notes describing the **blocking** for lines 308–333. You could use diagrams in your description.

One drop of Christian blood, thy lands and goods
Are by the laws of Venice confiscate
Unto the state of Venice.

Gratiano   O upright judge!
Mark, Jew. O learnèd judge!

Shylock   Is that the law?

Portia   Thyself shalt see the Act.   310
For as thou urgest justice, be assured
Thou shalt have justice, more than thou desirest.

Gratiano   O learnèd judge! Mark, Jew, a learnèd judge.

Shylock   I take this offer, then. Pay the bond thrice
And let the Christian go.

Bassanio   Here is the money.   315

Portia   Soft!
The Jew shall have all justice. Soft, no haste.
He shall have nothing but the penalty.

Gratiano   O, Jew, an upright judge, a learnèd judge.

Portia   Therefore prepare thee to cut off the flesh.   320
Shed thou no blood, nor cut thou less nor more
But just a pound of flesh. If thou tak'st more
Or less than a just pound, be it so much
As makes it light or heavy in the substance,
Or the division of the twentieth part   325
Of one poor scruple, nay, if the scale do turn
But in the estimation of a hair,
Thou diest and all thy goods are confiscate.

Gratiano   A second Daniel, a Daniel, Jew.
Now, infidel, I have thee on the hip.   330

Portia   Why doth the Jew pause? Take thy forfeiture.

Shylock   Give me my principal and let me go.

Bassanio   I have it ready for thee, here it is.

Shylock tries to leave the court, but Portia tells him to wait. She reveals what the law says: should a foreigner attempt to kill a Venetian citizen, his property is confiscated, with half going to the victim, half to the state. Also, the attempted murderer can be judged by the Duke of Venice, who can give the death penalty. The Duke spares Shylock's life.

Shylock and Portia, 2008

Activity 12: Exploring the action and the theme of justice

a. In groups, decide who will play Portia, the Duke of Venice, Gratiano, Antonio and Shylock. Read aloud lines 339–366.

b. Choose three moments you think tell the story of what happens in lines 339–366. Create three **freeze-frames** showing the characters as you think they would be at your chosen moments.

c. Say what Shylock is thinking in each freeze-frame.

d. Write a paragraph or two explaining what happens in lines 339–366. In your explanation, explore what Shylock is thinking at your chosen moments, including ideas about justice.

Glossary

342 **question** to argue
345 **alien** foreigner
348 **party** person
348 **contrive** plot
350 **privy coffer** private treasury
352 **'gainst... voice** despite any other appeals
358 **danger** damage
358 **rehearsed** declared

Key term

Freeze-frame a physical, still image created by people to represent an object, place, person or feeling

Portia	He hath refused it in the open court.
	He shall have merely justice and his bond. 335
Gratiano	A Daniel, still say I, a second Daniel.
	I thank thee, Jew, for teaching me that word.
Shylock	Shall I not have barely my principal?
Portia	Thou shalt have nothing but the forfeiture,
	To be taken so at thy peril, Jew. 340
Shylock	Why then the devil give him good of it.
	I'll stay no longer question.
Portia	Tarry, Jew.
	The law hath yet another hold on you.
	It is enacted in the laws of Venice,
	If it be proved against an alien 345
	That by direct or indirect attempts
	He seek the life of any citizen,
	The party 'gainst the which he doth contrive
	Shall seize one half his goods, the other half
	Comes to the privy coffer of the state, 350
	And the offender's life lies in the mercy
	Of the Duke only, 'gainst all other voice.
	In which predicament, I say, thou stand'st,
	For it appears, by manifest proceeding,
	That indirectly, and directly too, 355
	Thou hast contrived against the very life
	Of the defendant, and thou hast incurred
	The danger formerly by me rehearsed.
	Down therefore, and beg mercy of the Duke.
Gratiano	Beg that thou mayst have leave to hang thyself, 360
	And yet, thy wealth being forfeit to the state,
	Thou hast not left the value of a cord,
	Therefore thou must be hanged at the state's charge.
Duke	That thou shalt see the difference of our spirit,
	I pardon thee thy life before thou ask it. 365
	For half thy wealth, it is Antonio's,

The Duke says that if Shylock shows remorse, he can pay what he owes to the state as a fine. Antonio is willing to give up his half of the goods confiscated from Shylock on condition that Shylock leaves it to Lorenzo and Jessica when he dies. Also, Antonio demands that Shylock converts to Christianity. Shylock agrees.

Shylock, Portia, Servant, Bassanio, the Duke of Venice, Nerissa, Salerio, Gratiano and Antonio, 2011

Activity 13: Exploring the themes of the play

a. Read aloud lines 376–386. As you read:
   i. whenever you say 'I' or 'me', tap your chest
   ii. whenever you say 'he' or 'his', point to where Shylock could be in front of you
   iii. whenever you refer to Lorenzo or Jessica, point to where you imagine Belmont to be.

b. Discuss:
   i. how the play's themes of value, love and friendship, justice, fathers and daughters, and prejudice are reflected in these lines
   ii. how far you think Antonio is being merciful or vengeful in lines 376–386.

c. Write a paragraph that explains the ways in which the themes of the play are reflected in lines 376–386.

Glossary

368 **humbleness** remorse
375 **halter** rope to hang himself with
375 **gratis** free of interest
377 **quit** be satisfied with
378 **so** provided that
379 **use** legal trust
385 **all… possessed** everything he possesses when he dies
386 **son** i.e. son-in-law
387 **recant** withdraw
394 **godfathers** sponsors who ensure that a child is brought up as a Christian
395 **ten more** i.e. enough to make a jury of twelve

	The other half comes to the general state,	
	Which humbleness may drive unto a fine.	
Portia	Ay, for the state, not for Antonio.	
Shylock	Nay, take my life and all. Pardon not that.	370
	You take my house when you do take the prop	
	That doth sustain my house. You take my life	
	When you do take the means whereby I live.	
Portia	What mercy can you render him, Antonio?	
Gratiano	A halter gratis. Nothing else, for God's sake.	375
Antonio	So please my lord the Duke and all the court	
	To quit the fine for one half of his goods,	
	I am content, so he will let me have	
	The other half in use, to render it,	
	Upon his death, unto the gentleman	380
	That lately stole his daughter.	
	Two things provided more: that for this favour	
	He presently become a Christian;	
	The other, that he do record a gift	
	Here in the court of all he dies possessed	385
	Unto his son Lorenzo and his daughter.	
Duke	He shall do this, or else I do recant	
	The pardon that I late pronouncèd here.	
Portia	Art thou contented, Jew? What dost thou say?	
Shylock	I am content.	
Portia	Clerk, draw a deed of gift.	390
Shylock	I pray you give me leave to go from hence,	
	I am not well. Send the deed after me,	
	And I will sign it.	
Duke	Get thee gone, but do it.	
Gratiano	In christening thou shalt have two godfathers.	
	Had I been judge, thou shouldst have had ten more,	395

Shylock leaves, shortly followed by the Duke and his court, leaving Portia, who is still disguised as Balthasar, alone with Antonio and Bassanio. Bassanio tries to pay Balthasar, but Portia refuses. Bassanio offers a remembrance instead and Portia asks for the ring that she gave him.

Antonio and Bassanio, 2015

At the time

Using the context section on page 222, find out about the code of honour, to help you with the activity on this page.

Activity 14: Exploring honour

a. In groups, decide who will play Bassanio, Antonio and Portia. Remember, Portia is still disguised as Balthasar. Read aloud lines 404–425 three times:
   i.   as if Portia is trying to get away quickly so that the other characters do not see through her disguise
   ii. as if Portia is deliberately trying to get Bassanio to offer her the ring, to test the strength of his promise to her
   iii. as if Portia is jealous of Antonio and angry with Bassanio.
b. Using information you found for the 'At the time' task, discuss why you think Portia asks for the ring.
c. Write a paragraph that explores why Portia asks for the ring, including ideas about the themes of love, friendship and honour.

Glossary

396 **font** place of Christian baptism
400 **meet** necessary
401 **your... not** you do not have time to stay
402 **gratify** reward
405 **acquitted** freed
406 **in lieu whereof** in exchange for which
408 **cope** pay
408 **courteous pains** kind trouble
413 **account** consider; financially reckon
414 **mercenary** interested in money
417 **of... further** I must insist on giving you something
421 **You... far** you are very insistent

To bring thee to the gallows, not to the font.

Exit Shylock

Duke   Sir, I entreat you home with me to dinner.

Portia   I humbly do desire your grace of pardon.
I must away this night toward Padua,
And it is meet I presently set forth.   400

Duke   I am sorry that your leisure serves you not.
Antonio, gratify this gentleman,
For in my mind you are much bound to him.

Exit Duke and his train

Bassanio   Most worthy gentleman, I and my friend
Have by your wisdom been this day acquitted   405
Of grievous penalties, in lieu whereof
Three thousand ducats due unto the Jew
We freely cope your courteous pains withal.

Antonio   And stand indebted, over and above,
In love and service to you evermore.   410

Portia   He is well paid that is well satisfied,
And I, delivering you, am satisfied
And therein do account myself well paid.
My mind was never yet more mercenary.
I pray you know me when we meet again.   415
I wish you well, and so I take my leave.

Bassanio   Dear sir, of force I must attempt you further.
Take some remembrance of us as a tribute,
Not as fee. Grant me two things, I pray you:
Not to deny me, and to pardon me.   420

Portia   You press me far, and therefore I will yield.
Give me your gloves, I'll wear them for your sake.
And for your love, I'll take this ring from you.
Do not draw back your hand, I'll take no more,
And you in love shall not deny me this?   425

Bassanio explains that his wife gave him the ring and he has promised not to take it off. Balthasar appears unimpressed. She and Nerissa leave. Antonio persuades Bassanio to give the ring to Balthasar. Bassanio gives the ring to Gratiano so that he can run and give it to the lawyer.

Bassanio and Gratiano, 2008

Activity 15: Exploring the themes of love, friendship and value

a. In groups, decide who will play Portia, Bassanio, Nerissa, Gratiano and Antonio. Read aloud lines 426–453.

b. Stand in a circle, a few steps apart. To help you understand more about the characters, the relationships between them and their motives, read lines 426–453 again. This time, as you speak and listen, you should keep choosing between the following movements:
   - Take a step towards or away from another character.
   - Turn towards or away from another character.
   - Stand still.
   Try to make instinctive choices rather than planning what to do.

c. Discuss what love, friendship and value mean to these characters.

d. Look back over Act 4 Scene 1. Write a summary in the style of a blog of what happens in Act 4 Scene 1 from the point of view of the character you have been playing.

Glossary
429 **mind to** desire for
431 **dearest** most expensive
434 **liberal** free
440 **'scuse** excuse
453 **Fly** hasten

Bassanio	This ring, good sir, alas, it is a trifle;
	I will not shame myself to give you this.
Portia	I will have nothing else but only this,
	And now methinks I have a mind to it.
Bassanio	There's more depends on this than on the value.
	The dearest ring in Venice will I give you,
	And find it out by proclamation.
	Only for this, I pray you pardon me.
Portia	I see, sir, you are liberal in offers.
	You taught me first to beg, and now methinks
	You teach me how a beggar should be answered.
Bassanio	Good sir, this ring was given me by my wife,
	And when she put it on, she made me vow
	That I should neither sell nor give nor lose it.
Portia	That 'scuse serves many men to save their gifts.
	An if your wife be not a madwoman,
	And know how well I have deserved this ring,
	She would not hold out enemy forever
	For giving it to me. Well, peace be with you.

Exeunt Portia and Nerissa

Antonio	My Lord Bassanio, let him have the ring.
	Let his deservings and my love withal
	Be valued against your wife's commandment.
Bassanio	Go, Gratiano, run and overtake him.
	Give him the ring, and bring him, if thou canst,
	Unto Antonio's house. Away, make haste!

Exit Gratiano

Come, you and I will thither presently,
And in the morning early will we both
Fly toward Belmont. Come, Antonio.

Exeunt

430

435

440

445

450

Portia instructs Nerissa to take the deed of gift to Shylock's house for his signature before they return to Belmont that night. Gratiano catches them up and gives Balthasar the ring from Bassanio. Gratiano agrees to take Nerissa, who is still in disguise as a clerk, to Shylock's house. Nerissa discreetly tells her mistress that she will try to get the ring she gave to Gratiano as well.

Portia and Nerissa, 2008

At the time

Using the context section on page 220, remind yourself what the giving of a ring meant, to help you with the activity on this page.

Did you know?

Actors and their **director** experiment with different ways of staging a scene during rehearsals. There is no 'right' way of staging a scene. Actors experiment until they find the most effective way in order to help the audience understand what is going on.

Glossary

1 **Inquire... out** find out where Shylock's house is
3 **be** be there
5 **o'erta'en** overtaken
15 **Thou... warrant** I'm sure you will manage it
15 **old** extraordinary
17 **outface** defy; shame
18 **tarry** wait

Activity 1: Exploring an exit

a. In groups, decide who will play Portia, Nerissa and Gratiano. Read aloud lines 1–19.
b. Choose three moments you think tell the story of what happens in lines 1–19. Create three freeze-frames showing the characters as you think they would be at your chosen moments.
c. Using information you found for the 'At the time' task, say what your character is thinking in each freeze-frame.
d. Imagine you are the director of lines 1–19. Write director's notes describing how you think these lines should be staged and why.

Key term

Director the person who enables the practical and creative interpretation of a dramatic script, and ultimately brings together everybody's ideas in a way that engages the audience with the play

Act 4 | Scene 2

Enter Portia and Nerissa in disguise

Portia   Inquire the Jew's house out, give him this deed,
And let him sign it. We'll away tonight
And be a day before our husbands home.
This deed will be well welcome to Lorenzo.

Enter Gratiano

Gratiano   Fair sir, you are well o'erta'en.   5
My Lord Bassanio upon more advice
Hath sent you here this ring, and doth entreat
Your company at dinner.

Portia   That cannot be.
His ring I do accept most thankfully,
And so, I pray you tell him. Furthermore,   10
I pray you show my youth old Shylock's house.

Gratiano   That will I do.

Nerissa   Sir, I would speak with you.
[Aside to Portia] I'll see if I can get my husband's ring,
Which I did make him swear to keep forever.

Portia   [Aside to Nerissa] Thou mayst, I warrant. We shall have old swearing   15
That they did give the rings away to men,
But we'll outface them, and outswear them too.
Away, make haste. Thou know'st where I will tarry.

Nerissa   Come, good sir, will you show me to this house?

Exeunt

Exploring Act 4

Shylock, 2011

Activity 1: Exploring the action of Act 4

a. In groups, look back over Act 4.

b. Discuss what the people of Venice might be thinking about the events in the Duke's court.

c. One of you take on the role of producer of a news channel, while the others are journalists on your team or characters from Act 4.

d. Together, create a shooting script for a five-minute TV report about what has happened in Act 4. The shooting script should detail what happens and when during the report. It should include timings for each item in the report.

e. The report should include:
- footage of key events
- interviews with witnesses
- quotations from Act 4
- a summing-up of what you predict will happen next.

f. Film your five-minute report.

The Duke of Venice and Shylock, 2008

Gratiano, 2015

Activity 2: Exploring the language of Act 4

a. Select three moments from Act 4 where you feel the language is particularly interesting or powerful.

b. Explain the significance of the language in these moments, referring to specific details from the play. What does the language suggest about a particular character, theme or plot development?

In Belmont, Lorenzo and Jessica meet under the moon. They cite famous lovers as they discuss how they have come to be there together.

Jessica and Lorenzo, 2008

At the time

Using the context section on pages 220–221, find out how upper-class people arranged to meet those who they wanted to marry and what social rules governed courtship, to help you with the activity on this page.

Glossary

4 **Troilus** He was separated from his lover Cressida and later abandoned by her

7 **Thisbe** lover of Pyramus, who was scared away from their meeting place by a lion. Later they both killed themselves

7 **o'ertrip** skip over

10 **Dido** queen of Carthage who was abandoned by her lover Aeneas

10 **willow** symbol of lost love and grief

13 **Medea** She helped her lover Jason to get the golden fleece and restored the health of her father, Aeson

15 **steal** sneak away; rob

16 **unthrift** extravagant; penniless

19 **Stealing her soul** converting her from Judaism to Christianity, gaining her love

21 **shrew** scolding woman

Activity 1: Exploring the theme of value

a. In pairs, decide who will play Lorenzo and Jessica. Read aloud lines 1–22.

b. Read the lines again, as if the characters are in love, teasing each other.

c. Read the lines again, this time as if Jessica is regretting leaving her home and culture for Lorenzo, and Lorenzo is controlling Jessica.

d. Discuss how **tone**, **emphasis**, volume and **pace** help to bring out the **subtext** in task c.

e. Go through lines 1–22 and pick out all the words to do with danger or stealing.

f. Using information you found for the 'At the time' task, discuss what you think Jessica values at this point in the play.

Key terms

Themes the main ideas explored in a piece of literature, e.g. the themes of love and friendship, fathers and daughters, justice and mercy, prejudice, deceptive appearances and value might be considered key themes of *The Merchant of Venice*

Tone as in 'tone of voice'; expressing an attitude through how you say something

Emphasis stress given to words when speaking

Pace the speed at which someone speaks

Subtext the underlying meaning in the script

Act 5 | Scene 1

Enter Lorenzo and Jessica

Lorenzo The moon shines bright. In such a night as this,
When the sweet wind did gently kiss the trees
And they did make no noise, in such a night
Troilus methinks mounted the Trojan walls
And sighed his soul toward the Grecian tents   5
Where Cressid lay that night.

Jessica   In such a night
Did Thisbe fearfully o'ertrip the dew,
And saw the lion's shadow ere himself,
And ran dismayed away.

Lorenzo   In such a night
Stood Dido with a willow in her hand   10
Upon the wild sea banks and waft her love
To come again to Carthage.

Jessica   In such a night
Medea gathered the enchanted herbs
That did renew old Aeson.

Lorenzo   In such a night
Did Jessica steal from the wealthy Jew   15
And with an unthrift love did run from Venice
As far as Belmont.

Jessica   In such a night
Did young Lorenzo swear he loved her well,
Stealing her soul with many vows of faith,
And ne'er a true one.

Lorenzo   In such a night   20
Did pretty Jessica, like a little shrew,
Slander her love, and he forgave it her.

Stephano, a messenger from Portia, comes to let Lorenzo and Jessica know that Portia, Nerissa and a holy hermit will be returning to Belmont before morning. Lancelot lets them know that Bassanio will be back before morning.

Jessica and Lorenzo, 2015

Glossary

23 **out-night** i.e. beat you at this game
23 **did** if
24 **footing** footsteps
30 **doth stray about** is distracted by
31 **holy crosses** shrines by the side of the road
39 **Sola** imitation of a hunting cry
46 **post** messenger
46 **horn** cornucopia, horn full of plenty

Activity 2: Exploring staging choices

a. In groups, decide who will play Lorenzo, Jessica, Stephano and Lancelot. Read aloud lines 25–48.

b. Look back at the information you found for the 'At the time' task on page 68. Thinking about the kind of theatre *The Merchant of Venice* was first performed in, discuss the following:

   i. What clues are there in lines 25–48 that this scene happens at night?

   ii. The stage direction after line 24 is from the first published version of the play. Where do you think Stephano should enter the stage, and why?

   iii. At what point exactly during lines 39–48 do you think Lancelot and Lorenzo should see each other, and why?

   iv. How would you stage lines 25–48 to let the audience know that this scene happens at night?

c. Draw or write notes to describe what you have discussed in task b.

Key terms

Stage direction an instruction in the text of a play, e.g. indicating which characters enter and exit a scene

Dialogue a discussion between two or more people

Staging the process of selecting, adapting and developing the stage space in which a play will be performed

Jessica	I would out-night you, did nobody come.
	But hark, I hear the footing of a man.

Enter Stephano, a messenger

Lorenzo	Who comes so fast in silence of the night?	25
Stephano	A friend.	
Lorenzo	A friend? What friend? Your name, I pray you, friend?	
Stephano	Stephano is my name, and I bring word	
	My mistress will before the break of day	
	Be here at Belmont. She doth stray about	30
	By holy crosses, where she kneels and prays	
	For happy wedlock hours.	
Lorenzo	Who comes with her?	
Stephano	None but a holy hermit and her maid.	
	I pray you is my master yet returned?	
Lorenzo	He is not, nor we have not heard from him.	35
	But go we in, I pray thee, Jessica,	
	And ceremoniously let us prepare	
	Some welcome for the mistress of the house.	

Enter Lancelot

Lancelot	Sola, sola! Wo ha, ho! Sola, sola!	
Lorenzo	Who calls?	40
Lancelot	Sola! Did you see Master Lorenzo?	
	And Master Lorenzo, sola, sola!	
Lorenzo	Leave hollering, man, here.	
Lancelot	Sola! Where, where?	
Lorenzo	Here.	45
Lancelot	Tell him there's a post come from my master, with his horn full of	
	good news. My master will be here ere morning	
Lorenzo	Sweet soul, let's in, and there expect their coming.	

Lorenzo sends Stephano for musicians, who play. Lorenzo talks of the power of music to move people and tame wild horses. Jessica says she is never happy when she hears music.

Jessica and Lorenzo, 2011

Glossary

50 **signify** announce
52 **your music** the household musicians
58 **patens** shallow dishes for communion bread
61 **cherubins** Elizabethans imagined these as angelic, winged children
63 **muddy... decay** i.e. mortal clay, flesh
65 **Diana** the moon
69 **spirits** feelings
71 **race** herd
72 **Fetching** performing
76 **make... stand** all stand still together
77 **modest** gentle
78 **the poet** Ovid
79 **feign** invent
79 **Orpheus** in Greek myth, could charm all nature with his music

Activity 3: Exploring character – Jessica

a. Read line 68.
b. Create a **statue** of Jessica as she describes herself in line 68.
c. Write a list of everything that Jessica has lost in the play and another list of everything she has gained.
d. Discuss the photo of Jessica on this page. What mood do you think she is in, and why?
e. Write a paragraph explaining what Jessica says in line 68, using your lists and the photo on this page as inspiration.

Key terms

Statue like a freeze-frame but usually of a single character
Freeze-frame a physical, still image created by people to represent an object, place, person or feeling

And yet no matter. Why should we go in?
My friend Stephano, signify, pray you,   50
Within the house, your mistress is at hand,
And bring your music forth into the air.

Exit Stephano

How sweet the moonlight sleeps upon this bank.
Here will we sit and let the sounds of music
Creep in our ears. Soft stillness and the night   55
Become the touches of sweet harmony.
Sit, Jessica. Look how the floor of heaven
Is thick inlaid with patens of bright gold.
There's not the smallest orb which thou behold'st
But in his motion like an angel sings,   60
Still choiring to the young-eyed cherubins.
Such harmony is in immortal souls,
But whilst this muddy vesture of decay
Doth grossly close it in, we cannot hear it.

Enter Stephano with musicians

Come, ho, and wake Diana with a hymn.   65
With sweetest touches pierce your mistress' ear,
And draw her home with music.

Music plays

Jessica   I am never merry when I hear sweet music.

Lorenzo   The reason is your spirits are attentive.
For do but note a wild and wanton herd   70
Or race of youthful and unhandled colts,
Fetching mad bounds, bellowing and neighing loud,
Which is the hot condition of their blood.
If they but hear perchance a trumpet sound,
Or any air of music touch their ears,   75
You shall perceive them make a mutual stand,
Their savage eyes turned to a modest gaze
By the sweet power of music. Therefore the poet
Did feign that Orpheus drew trees, stones and floods,

Portia and Nerissa arrive home. The lights and music remind them how much they value Belmont after being in Venice and how much better things at home seem now they have been away.

Portia, 2015

Did you know?

The set designer for an RSC production produces detailed design notes and drawings. The designer first reads the script and picks up all the clues that are in it about the characters and the situation they are in. Then the designer considers the time period in which the production is set before producing their first drawings.

Glossary

80 **stockish** stupid
83 **concord** harmony
84 **stratagems** schemes
84 **spoils** destruction
86 **affections** feelings; disposition
86 **Erebus** a place of darkness in the classical underworld
90 **naughty** wicked
96 **main of waters** the sea
102 **attended** heard
106 **season** occasion
106 **seasoned** improved; flavoured
108 **Endymion** the shepherd who received the gift of eternal sleep from Diana, the moon goddess

Activity 4: Exploring setting

a. Read lines 88–90.
b. Imagine you are Portia, arriving home to Belmont on this night. Write down what you can see around you in as much detail as you can, using **adjectives** in your description. If you need inspiration, start with the light that is mentioned in line 88.
c. Do the same for the other senses of sound, smell and touch, then consider the overall **atmosphere**.
d. Write a detailed description of the setting for Act 5.
e. Look at the photo on this page. How have the **director** and designer of this production interpreted the setting for Act 5?

Key terms

Adjective a word that describes a noun, e.g. *blue, happy, big*
Atmosphere the mood created by staging choices
Director the person who enables the practical and creative interpretation of a dramatic script, and ultimately brings together everybody's ideas in a way that engages the audience with the play

Since nought so stockish, hard and full of rage,   80
But music for time doth change his nature.
The man that hath no music in himself,
Nor is not moved with concord of sweet sounds,
Is fit for treasons, stratagems and spoils.
The motions of his spirit are dull as night   85
And his affections dark as Erebus.
Let no such man be trusted. Mark the music.

Enter Portia and Nerissa

Portia   That light we see is burning in my hall.
How far that little candle throws his beams.
So shines a good deed in a naughty world.   90

Nerissa   When the moon shone, we did not see the candle.

Portia   So doth the greater glory dim the less.
A substitute shines brightly as a king
Until a king be by, and then his state
Empties itself, as doth an inland brook   95
Into the main of waters. Music, hark!

Nerissa   It is your music, madam, of the house.

Portia   Nothing is good, I see, without respect.
Methinks it sounds much sweeter than by day.

Nerissa   Silence bestows that virtue on it, madam.   100

Portia   The crow doth sing as sweetly as the lark
When neither is attended, and I think
The nightingale, if she should sing by day,
When every goose is cackling, would be thought
No better a musician than the wren.   105
How many things by season seasoned are
To their right praise and true perfection.
Peace! How the moon sleeps with Endymion
And would not be awaked.

Music ceases

Lorenzo welcomes Portia and Nerissa. A trumpet announces that Bassanio is approaching, and he returns to Belmont with Gratiano and Antonio. Bassanio asks Portia to welcome Antonio.

Bassanio and Portia, 2011

Bassanio and Portia, 2008

Activity 5: Exploring the theme of love and friendship

a. In groups, discuss what the audience knows about Portia that Bassanio and Antonio do not yet know.

b. Decide who will play Portia, Bassanio and Antonio. Read aloud lines 126–134 and then create a freeze-frame of the characters at this moment in the play.

c. Still in your group freeze-frame, take turns to speak aloud your thoughts, from the point of view of your character.

d. Look at the photos on this page, which show this moment in three different productions. Discuss what the characters are thinking.

e. Write a paragraph from the point of view of the character you have been playing, explaining what your hopes and fears are during lines 126–134. Include ideas about love and friendship.

Portia, Antonio, Bassanio and Gratiano, 2015

Lorenzo	That is the voice,
	Or I am much deceived, of Portia.

110

Portia	He knows me as the blind man knows the cuckoo,
	By the bad voice.

Lorenzo	Dear lady, welcome home.

Portia	We have been praying for our husbands' welfare,
	Which speed, we hope, the better for our words.
	Are they returned?

Lorenzo	Madam, they are not yet,

115

But there is come a messenger before
To signify their coming.

Portia	Go in, Nerissa.

Give order to my Servants that they take
No note at all of our being absent hence,
Nor you, Lorenzo, Jessica, nor you.

120

A tucket sounds

Lorenzo	Your husband is at hand, I hear his trumpet.
	We are no tell-tales, madam, fear you not.

Portia	This night methinks is but the daylight sick,
	It looks a little paler. 'Tis a day
	Such as the day is when the sun is hid.

125

Enter Bassanio, Antonio, Gratiano and their followers

Bassanio	We should hold day with the Antipodes,
	If you would walk in absence of the sun.

Portia	Let me give light, but let me not be light,
	For a light wife doth make a heavy husband,
	And never be Bassanio so for me,
	But God sort all. You are welcome home, my lord.

130

Bassanio	I thank you, madam. Give welcome to my friend.
	This is the man, this is Antonio,
	To whom I am so infinitely bound.

Portia welcomes Antonio. Nerissa and Gratiano quarrel because he no longer has the ring she gave him, having given it to the judge's clerk in Venice. Portia blames him for giving away his wife's first gift.

Nerissa, Servant and Gratiano, 2008

Activity 6: Exploring tactics

a. In pairs, decide who will play Gratiano and Nerissa. Read aloud lines 150–164.

b. Give the person playing Nerissa a handful of slips of paper. Read lines 150–164 again, this time Nerissa gives a slip of paper to Gratiano each time she says something that has an effect on him. Think about the **tactics** you use to give and receive the slips of paper. For example, on line 150, Nerissa might crumple up a slip of paper and throw it in Gratiano's face, or she might present it to him calmly. Gratiano might take it and throw it away casually, or he might put it in his pocket.

c. Write a paragraph that explains the tactics that Nerissa is using to trick Gratiano in lines 150–164.

Key term

Tactics the methods a character uses to get what they want

Portia	You should in all sense be much bound to him,	135
	For as I hear, he was much bound for you.	
Antonio	No more than I am well acquitted of.	
Portia	Sir, you are very welcome to our house.	
	It must appear in other ways than words,	
	Therefore I scant this breathing courtesy.	140
Gratiano	[To Nerissa] By yonder moon I swear you do me wrong.	
	In faith, I gave it to the judge's clerk.	
	Would he were gelt that had it, for my part,	
	Since you do take it, love, so much at heart.	
Portia	A quarrel, ho, already? What's the matter?	145
Gratiano	About a hoop of gold, a paltry ring	
	That she did give me, whose posy was	
	For all the world like cutler's poetry	
	Upon a knife, 'Love me, and leave me not'.	
Nerissa	What talk you of the posy or the value?	150
	You swore to me when I did give it you	
	That you would wear it till the hour of death,	
	And that it should lie with you in your grave.	
	Though not for me, yet for your vehement oaths,	
	You should have been respective and have kept it.	155
	Gave it a judge's clerk! But well I know	
	The clerk will ne'er wear hair on's face that had it.	
Gratiano	He will, and if he live to be a man.	
Nerissa	Ay, if a woman live to be a man.	
Gratiano	Now, by this hand, I gave it to a youth,	160
	A kind of boy, a little scrubbèd boy,	
	No higher than thyself, the judge's clerk,	
	A prating boy, that begged it as a fee.	
	I could not for my heart deny it him.	
Portia	You were to blame, I must be plain with you,	165
	To part so slightly with your wife's first gift,	

Portia says that if she found out that her husband had given her ring away, she would be angry. Gratiano reveals that Bassanio has given his ring away to Balthasar. Portia says she will not sleep with Bassanio until she sees the ring back on his finger and Nerissa says the same to Gratiano.

Key terms

Gesture a movement, often using the hands or head, to express a feeling or idea

Body language how we communicate feelings to each other using our bodies (including facial expressions) rather than words

Bassanio and Gratiano, 2011

Activity 7: Exploring the theme of value

a. In groups, decide who will play Bassanio, Gratiano, Portia and Nerissa. Read aloud lines 176–197.

b. Discuss:
   i. what Portia and Nerissa know that Bassanio and Gratiano do not know yet
   ii. what the value of their ring is to each character
   iii. why you think Shakespeare decided that Nerissa should give Gratiano a ring as well as Portia giving a ring to Bassanio.

c. Look through lines 176–197 again and reduce the scene to just 12 words. These can come from anywhere in those lines, including next to each other.

d. Create a performance of this moment in the play using only your 12 words, accompanied by actions and **gestures**. Your tone of voice and **body language** should tell the story of what happens clearly. Each character in the scene must respond to the words and actions of the other character.

e. Write a paragraph explaining what the value of their ring is for each character, using evidence from lines 176–197.

Glossary

171 **leave it** part with it
173 **masters** commands
175 **And 'twere to me** if it had happened to me
181 **pains** trouble
188 **void** empty

194

A thing stuck on with oaths upon your finger
And so riveted with faith unto your flesh.
I gave my love a ring and made him swear
Never to part with it, and here he stands. 170
I dare be sworn for him he would not leave it,
Nor pluck it from his finger for the wealth
That the world masters. Now, in faith, Gratiano,
You give your wife too unkind a cause of grief.
And 'twere to me, I should be mad at it. 175

Bassanio [Aside] Why I were best to cut my left hand off,
And swear I lost the ring defending it.

Gratiano My Lord Bassanio gave his ring away
Unto the judge that begged it and indeed
Deserved it too; and then the boy, his clerk, 180
That took some pains in writing, he begged mine,
And neither man nor master would take aught
But the two rings.

Portia What ring gave you, my lord?
Not that, I hope, which you received of me?

Bassanio If I could add a lie unto a fault, 185
I would deny it. But you see my finger
Hath not the ring upon it. It is gone.

Portia Even so void is your false heart of truth.
By heaven, I will ne'er come in your bed
Until I see the ring.

Nerissa Nor I in yours 190
Till I again see mine.

Bassanio Sweet Portia,
If you did know to whom I gave the ring,
If you did know for whom I gave the ring,
And would conceive for what I gave the ring,
And how unwillingly I left the ring, 195
When nought would be accepted but the ring,
You would abate the strength of your displeasure.

Portia berates Bassanio for giving the ring to someone else. Bassanio says that it was a matter of honour and, had Portia been there, she would have understood. Portia says that since Balthasar has the ring, she will be like Bassanio and not deny him (Balthasar) anything, even her bed.

Bassanio and Portia, 2008

Glossary

198 **virtue** power
200 **contain** keep
204 **terms of zeal** determination
204 **wanted** lacked
204 **modesty** restraint
205 **ceremony** sacred token
207 **I'll... for't** I would die for my belief
209 **civil doctor** doctor of civil law
218 **besmear** stain
219 **candles... night** stars
229 **Argus** monster with a hundred eyes

Activity 8: Exploring the theme of deceptive appearances

a. In pairs, decide who will play Portia and Bassanio. Read aloud lines 208–232.
b. Look at the photo on this page of Portia and Bassanio. Which line from lines 208–232 do you think is being spoken in this photo? Explain your reasons.
c. Write one sentence to explain each of the following:
   i. how what happens in lines 208–232 helps to develop the theme of deceptive appearances
   ii. how what happens helps to create **dramatic tension**.

Key term

Dramatic tension the anticipation of an outcome on stage, keeping the audience in suspense

Portia	If you had known the virtue of the ring,	
	Or half her worthiness that gave the ring,	
	Or your own honour to contain the ring,	200
	You would not then have parted with the ring.	
	What man is there so much unreasonable,	
	If you had pleased to have defended it	
	With any terms of zeal, wanted the modesty	
	To urge the thing held as a ceremony?	205
	Nerissa teaches me what to believe,	
	I'll die for't but some woman had the ring.	
Bassanio	No, by mine honour, madam, by my soul,	
	No woman had it, but a civil doctor,	
	Which did refuse three thousand ducats of me	210
	And begged the ring, the which I did deny him	
	And suffered him to go displeased away,	
	Even he that had held up the very life	
	Of my dear friend. What should I say, sweet lady?	
	I was enforced to send it after him.	215
	I was beset with shame and courtesy.	
	My honour would not let ingratitude	
	So much besmear it. Pardon me, good lady,	
	And by these blessèd candles of the night,	
	Had you been there, I think you would have begged	220
	The ring of me to give the worthy doctor.	
Portia	Let not that doctor e'er come near my house.	
	Since he hath got the jewel that I loved,	
	And that which you did swear to keep for me,	
	I will become as liberal as you.	225
	I'll not deny him anything I have,	
	No, not my body nor my husband's bed.	
	Know him I shall, I am well sure of it.	
	Lie not a night from home. Watch me like Argus.	
	If you do not, if I be left alone,	230
	Now by mine honour, which is yet mine own,	
	I'll have the doctor for my bedfellow.	
Nerissa	And I his clerk. Therefore be well advised	

Antonio says he is upset that he is the cause of the quarrel. Bassanio swears he will never break a promise to Portia again. Portia gives Antonio the ring to give to Bassanio. Bassanio realises that it is the same ring that he gave to Balthasar.

Antonio, Portia and Bassanio, 2011

Activity 9: Exploring the themes of love, friendship, deceptive appearances and value

a. In groups, decide who will play Antonio, Portia, Bassanio and Nerissa. Read aloud lines 237–261.

b. Read the lines again, but this time whisper them as if the characters are talking about something secret and do not want to be overheard.

c. Stand about five steps apart and read the lines again, loudly.

d. Discuss how these different ways of reading change your understanding of the lines.

e. Finally, read the lines again, this time varying the volume of your speech according to how you think they should be performed. Discuss:

   i. how you think the characters are feeling during lines 237–261

   ii. why Portia says she has slept with Balthasar on line 258.

f. Write a paragraph explaining why you think Shakespeare included this scene in the play and how it contributes to the themes of love, friendship, deceptive appearances and value.

Glossary

235 **take** catch
236 **mar... pen** I'll ruin his equipment
244 **double** two-faced; two-fold
245 **of credit** worth believing
250 **quite miscarried** been completely lost
252 **advisedly** deliberately
261 **In lieu of** in exchange for

How you do leave me to mine own protection.

Gratiano	Well, do you so. Let not me take him, then.	235
	For if I do, I'll mar the young clerk's pen.	

Antonio   I am th'unhappy subject of these quarrels.

Portia   Sir, grieve not you. You are welcome notwithstanding.

Bassanio   Portia, forgive me this enforcèd wrong,
And in the hearing of these many friends,   240
I swear to thee, even by thine own fair eyes,
Wherein I see myself—

Portia   Mark you but that?
In both my eyes he doubly sees himself,
In each eye, one. Swear by your double self,
And there's an oath of credit.

Bassanio   Nay, but hear me.   245
Pardon this fault, and by my soul I swear
I never more will break an oath with thee.

Antonio   I once did lend my body for thy wealth,
Which but for him that had your husband's ring,
Had quite miscarried. I dare be bound again,   250
My soul upon the forfeit, that your lord
Will never more break faith advisedly.

Portia   Then you shall be his surety. Give him this
And bid him keep it better than the other.

Antonio   Here, Lord Bassanio, swear to keep this ring.   255

Bassanio   By heaven, it is the same I gave the doctor.

Portia   I had it of him. Pardon, Bassanio,
For, by this ring, the doctor lay with me.

Nerissa   And pardon me, my gentle Gratiano,
For that same scrubbèd boy, the doctor's clerk,   260
In lieu of this last night did lie with me.

Gratiano   Why this is like the mending of highways

Portia reveals that she was Balthasar and Nerissa was the clerk. She explains that she has just arrived back from Venice. She has a letter for Antonio, which says that three of his merchant ships have unexpectedly returned to Venice. Nerissa gives Lorenzo the deed of gift from Shylock.

Antonio, Bassanio and Gratiano, 2008

Activity 10: Exploring status

a. Read lines 265–278.
b. Go back through Act 5 and list all the characters that are on stage at this moment.
c. Put the list in order of most important to least important, then most respected to least respected at this moment.
d. What were the differences between your lists? Status is made up of a combination of social and personal power. Which character do you think has the highest status during lines 265–278? Give reasons for your answer.
e. Choose any of the characters on your list other than Portia. Imagining you are your chosen character, write a letter to Portia telling her what you think of her at this moment, using information you found for the 'At the time' task.

At the time

Using the context section on page 222, remind yourself of the social status of women, to help you with the activity on this page.

Glossary

264 **cuckolds** men whose wives are unfaithful to them
265 **grossly** crudely
271 **e'en** just
276 **richly** full of expensive goods
285 **living** livelihood
287 **road** harbour

	In summer, where the ways are fair enough.	
	What, are we cuckolds ere we have deserved it?	
Portia	Speak not so grossly. You are all amazed.	265
	Here is a letter, read it at your leisure.	
	It comes from Padua, from Bellario.	
	There you shall find that Portia was the doctor,	
	Nerissa there her clerk. Lorenzo here	
	Shall witness I set forth as soon as you,	270
	And but e'en now returned; I have not yet	
	Entered my house. Antonio, you are welcome,	
	And I have better news in store for you	
	Than you expect. Unseal this letter soon.	
	There you shall find three of your argosies	275
	Are richly come to harbour suddenly.	
	You shall not know by what strange accident	
	I chancèd on this letter.	
Antonio	I am dumb.	
Bassanio	Were you the doctor and I knew you not?	
Gratiano	Were you the clerk that is to make me cuckold?	280
Nerissa	Ay, but the clerk that never means to do it,	
	Unless he live until he be a man.	
Bassanio	Sweet doctor, you shall be my bedfellow.	
	When I am absent, then lie with my wife.	
Antonio	Sweet lady, you have given me life and living,	285
	For here I read for certain that my ships	
	Are safely come to road.	
Portia	How now, Lorenzo?	
	My clerk hath some good comforts too for you.	
Nerissa	Ay, and I'll give them him without a fee.	
	There do I give to you and Jessica,	290
	From the rich Jew, a special deed of gift,	
	After his death, of all he dies possessed of.	

Portia invites everyone in for their questions to be answered. Gratiano looks forward to celebrating with Nerissa.

Antonio, Portia, Bassanio and Jessica, 2011

Did you know?

Shakespeare's plays are often classified as comedies or tragedies. *The Merchant of Venice* is classified as a comedy because the ending is considered to be a happy one, but there are things that happen in the play that are very serious for the characters involved. Some productions choose to emphasise the darker side of the play as opposed to treating it as pure comedy.

At the time

Using the context section on page 216, find out what the traditional ending of a comedy was, to help you with the activity on this page.

Activity 11: Exploring the themes of the play

a. Read lines 294–298.
b. Discuss the ways in which the events of the play have changed the relationships between the characters.
c. Write a question in modern English that each character might have at the end of the play.
d. Using information you found for the 'At the time' task, write a paragraph that discusses the extent to which the ending of the play makes it a traditional comedy. Include your suggestions for how a modern audience might feel watching the end of the play.

Glossary

293 **manna** in the Bible, the food from heaven that saved the Israelites from starving in the desert
296 **at full** in detail
297 **charge... inter'gatories** interrogate us under oath
304 **couching** going to bed with
305–306 **I'll... sore** I'll take care of nothing so much

Lorenzo	Fair ladies, you drop manna in the way Of starvèd people.
Portia	It is almost morning, And yet I am sure you are not satisfied Of these events at full. Let us go in, And charge us there upon inter'gatories, And we will answer all things faithfully.
Gratiano	Let it be so. The first inter'gatory That my Nerissa shall be sworn on is Whether till the next night she had rather stay, Or go to bed now, being two hours to day. But were the day come, I should wish it dark, Till I were couching with the doctor's clerk. Well, while I live I'll fear no other thing So sore as keeping safe Nerissa's ring.

295

300

305

Exeunt

Exploring Act 5

Gratiano, Portia, Bassanio, Jessica, Lorenzo and the company, 2008

Activity 1: Exploring the action of Act 5

a. In groups, look back over Act 5. Use the page summaries to prepare an engaging short performance of the whole act.

b. One person in your group reads the page summaries aloud, while the rest of the group acts out everything that happens in the most exaggerated way that they can. You can use single words or short lines from the text to help your performance. For example, on page 182, the page summary mentions that Lorenzo and Jessica meet under the moon. You might choose one or two of the things that they say on page 183 to be part of your performance

Portia, 2011

Activity 2: Exploring the end of the play

In groups, look back over Act 5, remembering all the things that have happened. Use the page summaries to help you. Remind yourself of the key points that have happened earlier in the play as well. Imagine that the events of Act 5 have taken place today and the double wedding of Portia and Bassanio, Nerissa and Gratiano is to be featured on the TV news. Your job is to produce that TV news feature.

a. Choose two people to be the presenters of the programme and one person to be a reporter on location at Belmont. The rest of you can be characters from the play. Bear in mind that Shylock does not appear in Act 5. Discuss why Shakespeare might have left Shylock out of the ending, and use your ideas to decide if and how you are going to include Shylock in the news feature.

b. You should report on the wedding itself, but your programme must include as much detail as possible about what has happened in the play and interviews with the characters of your choice. You must include a variety of characters with different points of view and use quotations from the play.

c. Put your programme together to share with the rest of your class.

Exploring the play

Portia, 2011

Activity 1: Exploring the themes of the play

a. Choose one of the following themes:
   - Justice and mercy
   - Value
   - Love and friendship
   - Prejudice
   - Deceptive appearances
   - Fathers and daughters
   i.   Look back over Act 5 and trace how ideas about your chosen theme are developed and resolved in Act 5.
   ii. Identify the characters linked to this theme, and explore how their words and actions express ideas about it.
b. Either prepare a presentation or write an essay about your chosen theme, entitled 'Discuss whether the theme of _____ is successfully concluded in Act 5'.

Activity 2: Assessing the relevance of the play

Look at the photos on these pages. In these productions, the directors wanted the audience to explore the themes of the play in a contemporary context, and draw parallels between the events of the play and events in the modern world.

a. Discuss the following questions:

   i. Which of the things that happen in the play could happen now? Why do you think that?

   ii. What do you learn about justice and mercy through studying this play?

   iii. What do you think is the main message of this play?

   iv. Why do you think the play is considered to be worth studying in this day and age?

b. Following your discussion, write an essay with the title: 'How is Shakespeare's play *The Merchant of Venice* still relevant today?' Use the questions in task a to structure your essay into four paragraphs.

Jessica and Lorenzo, 2008

William Shakespeare and his world

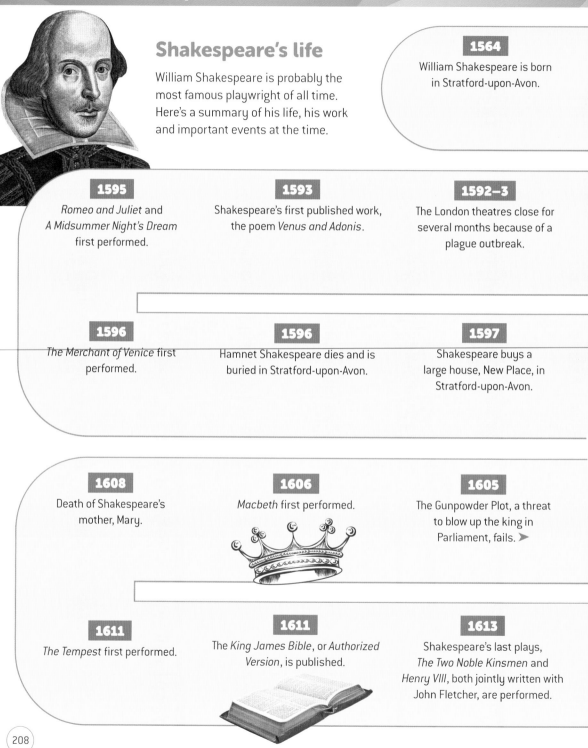

Shakespeare's life

William Shakespeare is probably the most famous playwright of all time. Here's a summary of his life, his work and important events at the time.

1564
William Shakespeare is born in Stratford-upon-Avon.

1595
Romeo and Juliet and A Midsummer Night's Dream first performed.

1593
Shakespeare's first published work, the poem Venus and Adonis.

1592–3
The London theatres close for several months because of a plague outbreak.

1596
The Merchant of Venice first performed.

1596
Hamnet Shakespeare dies and is buried in Stratford-upon-Avon.

1597
Shakespeare buys a large house, New Place, in Stratford-upon-Avon.

1608
Death of Shakespeare's mother, Mary.

1606
Macbeth first performed.

1605
The Gunpowder Plot, a threat to blow up the king in Parliament, fails. ➤

1611
The Tempest first performed.

1611
The King James Bible, or Authorized Version, is published.

1613
Shakespeare's last plays, The Two Noble Kinsmen and Henry VIII, both jointly written with John Fletcher, are performed.

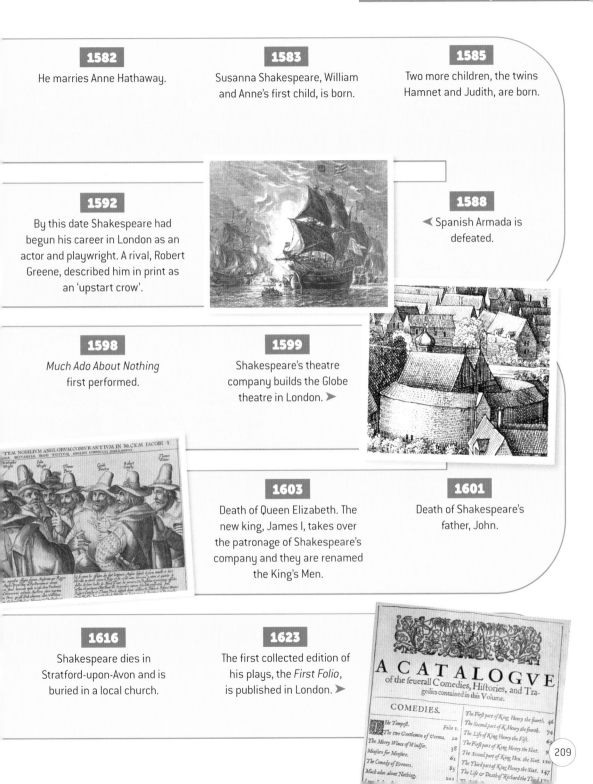

1582

He marries Anne Hathaway.

1583

Susanna Shakespeare, William and Anne's first child, is born.

1585

Two more children, the twins Hamnet and Judith, are born.

1592

By this date Shakespeare had begun his career in London as an actor and playwright. A rival, Robert Greene, described him in print as an 'upstart crow'.

1588

◀ Spanish Armada is defeated.

1598

Much Ado About Nothing first performed.

1599

Shakespeare's theatre company builds the Globe theatre in London. ➤

1603

Death of Queen Elizabeth. The new king, James I, takes over the patronage of Shakespeare's company and they are renamed the King's Men.

1601

Death of Shakespeare's father, John.

1616

Shakespeare dies in Stratford-upon-Avon and is buried in a local church.

1623

The first collected edition of his plays, the *First Folio*, is published in London. ➤

A CATALOGVE of the feuerall Comedies, Histories, and Tragedies contained in this Volume.

COMEDIES.

The Tempest. Folio 1.
The two Gentlemen of Verona. 20
The Merry Wiues of Windsor. 38
Measure for Measure. 61
The Comedy of Errours. 85
Much adoo about Nothing. 101

The First part of King Henry the fourth. 46
The Second part of K. Henry the fourth. 74
The Life of King Henry the Fift. 69
The First part of King Henry the Sixt. 96
The Second part of King Hen. the Sixt. 120
The Third part of King Henry the Sixt. 147
The Life & Death of Richard the Third.

209

Shakespeare's language

Shakespeare's language can be difficult for us to understand for two different reasons. One is historical: words and their meanings, and the ways people express themselves, have changed over the four hundred years since he wrote. The other is poetic: Shakespeare's characters don't speak like ordinary people, even in the Elizabethan period, would have spoken. They speak in a heightened, poetic language full of repetition and elaboration.

Verse and prose

Most Shakespeare plays are written in verse with a small proportion of prose included. You can tell verse from prose on the page because verse lines are usually shorter and each line begins with a capital letter, whereas prose lines usually begin with lower-case letters (unless it is the beginning of a sentence) and continue to the very edge of the paper. Verse is a more formal way of speaking and is often associated with higher-status characters, whereas servants or other lower-class figures more often speak prose. Comic scenes are sometimes in prose, where the language is more relaxed and natural.

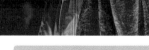

Antonio and Bassanio, 2015

Shakespeare's verse is often called blank verse – blank means it does not rhyme. But occasionally he does use rhyme, sometimes in a couplet (two rhyming lines) at the end of a scene to signal that it has come to a conclusion. For example, here's Antonio's cheerful ending to Act 1 Scene 3 in which he borrows money from Shylock:

Antonio	Come on, in this there can be no dismay.
	My ships come home a month before the day.

At other times, Shakespeare uses rhyme to suggest formality. Rhyming lines were probably easier for actors to learn.

Iambic pentameter

Poetry – like music – is words ordered into rhythm. The metre of poetry is like its drumbeat. Most of Shakespeare's verse lines are written in iambic pentameter. A pentameter means that there are five beats to the line (and usually ten syllables); iambic means that the beats are alternately weak and strong, or unstressed and stressed.

An example from *The Merchant of Venice* is Antonio's first line in the play, below. The numbers below the line count the syllables; the marks below that show that the syllables alternate between unstressed (signalled with -) and stressed (/). It looks more complicated when you write it down than when you read it aloud.

Antonio	In sooth I know not why I am so sad.
	1 2 3 4 5 6 7 8 9 10
	- / - / - / - / - /

As with music, the sound of Shakespeare's language would get repetitive if he never varied the rhythm. So sometimes he changes the arrangement of stressed and unstressed syllables, and sometimes lines can be read with different emphases depending on the actor's interpretation. Reading Shakespeare's lines aloud often helps.

One clue: often Shakespeare puts important words or ideas at the end of his lines, rather than at the beginning. If you look down a speech and look at the last word in each line you can usually get some idea of the main point of the speech. One additional clue: with longer speeches, often the beginning and the end are the most important, and the middle says the same thing in different ways.

Shakespeare's World

Knowing something about life in Shakespeare's England is often helpful for our understanding of his plots and characters, and of the assumptions that members of his audiences would have had when they went to see his plays. But it is also important to remember that he was an imaginative playwright, making up stories for entertainment.

Just as we wouldn't necessarily rely on modern Hollywood films or television drama to depict our everyday reality, so too we need sometimes to acknowledge that Shakespeare is showing his audiences something exotic, unfamiliar or fairy tale.

London

At some point in his early twenties, Shakespeare moved from the country town of Stratford to London. Thousands of people at the time did the same, moving to the city for work and other opportunities, and London expanded rapidly during the Elizabethan and Jacobean periods. It was a busy, commercial place that had outgrown the original walled city and was now organised around the main thoroughfare, the river Thames. Shakespeare never sets a play in contemporary London, although many of his urban locations, particularly Venice, seem to recall the inns and streets and bustle of the city in which he and his audiences lived and worked.

17th-century engraving of London by Claes Jansz Visscher

As a port city, London was a place where people from different places mixed together, although its society was much less racially diverse than now. Jews had been banned from England in the medieval period, although there were some secret communities in London, so almost no one in Shakespeare's England would ever have met a Jewish person. A visit of Arab ambassadors from North Africa to Queen Elizabeth's court in 1600 must have seemed very exotic indeed.

Venice

In Shakespeare's time, Venice was a prosperous commercial city with very strong trading connections to the east. Ships went from the city – organized around a network of canals and waterways – across the Mediterranean to Turkey, India and beyond, bringing back expensive and exotic items such as spices and silks. There was risk involved – such as the threat of poor sailing conditions and possible shipwreck – but big profits could be made by bringing back rare goods to sell in the city. Venice was a melting pot of items and people from different countries and races and religions.

The Duke of Venice, *The Merchant of Venice*, 2015

For some people in Shakespeare's time, Venice was a model for London: both cities were organized around the water and were wealthy centres of trade, with formal legal systems. The court scene in the play is probably a mixture of English and Venetian law: Shakespeare's audiences, many of them legal students, were interested in seeing court scenes on stage, and he often includes them in his plays. The play also combines the awareness that Venice had some particular laws to govern its own cosmopolitan population, and the common feature of comedy, that a ruler or governor exercises mercy over prisoners. Often Shakespeare sets his plays in places that are partly foreign and partly more familiar and local. We don't know whether he ever travelled to Venice, but in any case, apart from the mention of the famous landmark the Rialto Bridge, there is not very much detail about the city. He probably read about it in his sources.

Shakespeare's company and the theatre

When he wrote *The Merchant of Venice*, Shakespeare was an actor, the chief playwright and an investor in a company of actors called the Lord Chamberlain's Men. The company in London in an open-air theatre with a large yard for standing audience members and tiered seating round the outside.

Theatres in Shakespeare's time did not have very elaborate scenery – you can perform *The Merchant of Venice* with just a few props – and they tended to describe the setting rather than show it. In Act 1 Scene 1 for example, there are lots of mentions of shipping and the types of business that were so important to Venice, establishing the setting without actually showing it visually. Plays were performed in the afternoon, as there was no artificial lighting to light the stage at night. So if a scene was set at night, for instance, it was not possible to lower the lights to suggest darkness. Instead, the actors would carry lanterns or other lights, even though it was broad daylight, to signal that this was a night scene. Audiences needed to bring their imaginations to the theatre.

The modern Globe Theatre in London is modelled on the theatre that Shakespeare's company built in 1599

Shakespeare's acting troupe, the Lord Chamberlain's Men, was probably twelve or fourteen men (male actors played all the roles including female ones), so they also doubled up and played more than one part. It is likely that most costumes were the Elizabethan equivalent of 'modern dress': so that actors were wearing clothes similar to those around the audience and the London streets. Some characters' costumes were designed to be deliberately showy: we can see in the original stage direction for the entrance of the Prince of Morocco 'all in white, and three or four followers accordingly', that this might have been a spectacular stage image that suggested exotic wealth (only a very rich person would have white clothes).

The audience for Shakespeare's plays was quite mixed, but probably tended to be younger rather than older and male rather than female. Entry to the theatres was cheap — one penny, the cost of two pints of beer — so a relatively diverse social mix could attend. We don't know how well-educated the audience was, although educational opportunities were expanding during the sixteenth century and historians think that male literacy levels in London at this point may have been as high as 50%. Literacy was connected to social status: wealthier individuals were much more likely to be educated than poorer ones. But more people went to see Shakespeare's plays in the theatre than read them when they were printed.

The 'Flower' portrait of Shakespeare, c. 1830

Comedy and tragedy

For us, a comedy is something funny. In Shakespeare's time, comedy had those associations too, but more importantly it was defined by the shape of the story. A comedy had a happy ending, in which characters were united, social bonds reaffirmed and things were better than they were at the beginning. A tragedy was the opposite: the central tragic character (often the play is named after them) becomes more and more isolated and is destroyed in a plot where things are definitely worse at the end than at the beginning. One of Shakespeare's fellow playwrights, Thomas Heywood, defined comedy and tragedy: 'comedies begin in trouble and end in peace; tragedies begin in calms and end in tempest'.

Comedies traditionally ended with reunion or with marriage. Those elements that kept the couple apart during the play – sometimes these are external factors such as a disapproving parent, sometimes more psychological factors such as an unwillingness to commit – are overcome. The final scene of a comedy tends to bring together all its characters and reconcile all the plots. The suggestion is that the new couples will bring about new life and the regeneration of the community.

Puck, *A Midsummer Night's Dream*, 1954

Shakespeare's sources

Shakespeare read lots of different works that had a direct or indirect influence on his plays. There are lots of legends and folktales that tell the story of a loan where human flesh is the security, including an Italian story in which a merchant borrows money from a Jewish moneylender on behalf of his godson, who goes off to seek a bride. Shakespeare got the story of the three caskets – the competition to win Portia's hand in marriage – from a collection of tales called the *Gesta Romanorum*. The characters of Shylock and Jessica may have been influenced by Shakespeare's fellow playwright Christopher Marlowe, whose popular play *The Jew of Malta* featured Barabas, an amoral and scheming miser with a daughter called Abigail.

Barabas and Abigail, *The Jew of Malta*, 2015

Fate

Many people in Elizabethan England believed in Fate, and in horoscopes and the idea that the position of the planets at the time of birth influenced the child's future life. Astronomical events like solar or lunar eclipses or comets visible in the sky were often understood to be signs or portents. The planets were also thought to have a role in disease: the word 'influenza' (from which we get the abbreviation 'flu') comes from the Latin for astrological influence. These older, more superstitious attitudes to the planets coexisted in Shakespeare's lifetime with the new scientific discoveries including Galileo's telescope and observations of the planets by other astronomers.

Religion and race

One of the features of Venice in the sixteenth century was that it was a cosmopolitan and diverse city with a mixture of races and religions living and trading. Travellers to the city commented on the gated area where the Jews lived, which was called the ghetto. Since then, the word 'ghetto' has been used in many different countries to describe areas of a city where a minority group lives. Although there were differences between the different peoples in the city, trade and business tied them together in economic relationships. However, it would have been very unusual for people of different religions to marry each other at this time. Because the Bible suggested that it was wrong for Christians to charge interest on loans, Jews were particularly associated with moneylending or usury, which was an important aspect of Venetian business life.

There were no Jewish people living openly in England at the time Shakespeare wrote this play, and he may well never have met a Jewish person: Shylock is a made-up creation based on partial ideas and negative stereotypes, even if he also challenges that stereotype. Many people believed that the Jewish people would never convert to Christianity: it is not quite clear at the end of the play whether Shylock and Jessica convert under pressure from the Christian authorities. When Shakespeare wrote the play, Shylock may have been seen as a comic character, but more recent actors have brought out the suffering in his role, particularly drawing on the history of Jewish persecution. Some people, including the modern playwright Arnold Wesker, think that it would be better not to perform *The Merchant of Venice* because it is racially prejudiced. Certainly it is true in the court scene that the law of Venice seems to treat Christians and Jews differently.

Portia's suitor the Prince of Morocco represents another ethnic group. In Elizabethan England the word 'Moor' referred to a Muslim, probably from North Africa. Moors were important business partners, and good relations with them were key to the Venetian trading economy. The records show us that there were a few people of Muslim or Moorish origin living in London: they probably seen as strange and unusual.

Henry Urwick (1859–1931) as Shylock, oil on canvas by Walter Chamberlain Urwick

Love

Romantic love had been a prominent literary theme for centuries. Courtly love traditions tended to present an idealised female figure who ignored her suffering admirer; romantic stories tended to end in disappointment or worse. Love was considered to be a random emotion (in contrast to the arranged marriages discussed under 'marriage and courtship' on page 220). The symbolism of the blindfolded god of love, Cupid, was clear: Love did not care where his arrows fell, creating mayhem in the world by making people fall in love with each other. The goddess of sexual love, Venus, was well-known in Elizabethan literature: one of Shakespeare's earliest works is a long poem, *Venus and Adonis*, which flips the usual story for comic effect and shows the goddess longing for a young man who is not interested in her.

Claudio and Hero, *Much Ado About Nothing*, 1950

A person in love was often thought to show symptoms of melancholy or depression, and to withdraw from company, particularly of the same sex. Enjoying love poetry or other romantic literature, or the company of women (for men) might also be a sign of being in love.

Marriage and courtship

Elizabethan marriages tended to be seen as alliances between families, as much as between the couple themselves. In wealthy or noble families, a suitable marriage arranged between the parents of the couple was common, and often the couple themselves would spend little or no time alone together before their marriage; for ordinary people, there may have been more possibility to choose a partner, although parental permission was still important.

For Jessica and for Portia in *The Merchant of Venice*, their fathers attempt to control their marriage choices. Once they were married, women had to obey their husbands: a married woman — like the wealthy Portia — could not use her money independently. The exchanging of rings was a common token of commitment: and exchanging rings in front of a witness and promising to marry was seen as a formal, binding agreement between the couple.

Rose Oatley, Sir Hugh Lacy and Rowland Lacy, *The Shoemaker's Holiday*, 2014

Marriage was a practical commitment rather than, or as well as, a romantic partnership: perhaps couples then did not place such high emotional expectations on their married relationships as in modern western societies. Instead, emotionally intense friendships between men had a high social status. One writer from the same time as Shakespeare described a 'faithful friend' as 'an alter ego, that is, another himself'. Perhaps this explains Antonio's self-sacrificing generosity to his friend – but recent critics have suggested that he is in love with Bassanio. Despite being illegal, romantic love between men was a feature of the Elizabethan period too, and among his sonnets Shakespeare wrote a number of love poems to an adored young man. It may be that Antonio's sadness at the beginning of the play is bound up with a sense that in his society he cannot have what he truly wants.

Falstaff's Page and Doll Tearsheet, *Henry IV Part 2*, 2014

Children

In the Elizabethan period, children were expected to obey their parents, wives their husbands, and servants their masters. Consequences of disobedience could be very serious. Children in higher-class families often lived with relatives or were quite distant from their parents; for lower-status families, young children would be expected to work in the household. It is likely that the young Shakespeare would have helped out in his father's workshop. Young children in noble families wore the same clothes for both sexes until a ceremony called 'breeching' when boys began to wear breeches (trousers), aged about 7.

Women

Ideas about the ideal woman are current in many societies, including modern ones. Just as we know that most real women now do not conform to the thin, beautiful, youthful ideal of modern advertising, so too probably Elizabethan women were different from the models given to them in conduct books, sermons and literature. The ideal woman, according to writers on morality in Shakespeare's England, remained meekly at home. She was chaste, honest, silent and obedient to her husband's will.

A moral double standard meant that women's behaviour, especially their chastity, was much more policed than that of men. Unmarried women were expected to obey their fathers and conduct themselves modestly. Women did not attend school or university, although wealthy ones might be educated at home. Except for widows, women could not hold property in their own right. But alongside these stereotypes there were many exceptional women, from Queen Elizabeth to the writer Mary Sidney and the pirate Mary Killigrew, as well as ordinary women living, working and running their households.

Bianca, *Love's Sacrifice*, 2015

Honour

Behaving honourably was an important element of male and female behaviour. But male and female honour were differently understood. For men, honour was about status and about being judged by others: keeping up appearances, looking brave and manly, not being ridiculed or made to look foolish. For women, honour was about sexual conduct: to be honourable was to be chaste and to be seen to be chaste. Honourable behaviour for women was to be beyond reproach.

Key terms glossary

Adjective a word that describes a noun, e.g. *blue*, *happy*, *big*

Antithesis bringing two opposing concepts or ideas together, e.g. hot and cold, love and hate, loud and quiet

Aside when a character addresses a remark to the audience that other characters on the stage do not hear

Atmosphere the mood created by staging choices

Back-story what happened to any of the characters before the start of the play

Banter playful dialogue where the speakers verbally score points off each other

Blocking the movements agreed for staging a scene

Body language how we communicate feelings to each other using our bodies (including facial expressions) rather than words

Dialogue a discussion between two or more people

Director the person who enables the practical and creative interpretation of a dramatic script, and ultimately brings together everybody's ideas in a way that engages the audience with the play

Dramatic tension the anticipation of an outcome on stage, keeping the audience in suspense

Emphasis stress given to words when speaking

Extended metaphor describing something by comparing it to something else over several lines

Freeze-frame a physical, still image created by people to represent an object, place, person or feeling

Gesture a movement, often using the hands or head, to express a feeling or idea

Iambic pentameter the rhythm Shakespeare uses to write his plays. Each line in this rhythm contains approximately ten syllables. 'Iambic' means putting the stress on the second syllable of each beat. 'Pentameter' means five beats with two syllables in each beat

Imagery visually descriptive language

Improvise make up in the moment

Malapropism mistaken use of a word that sounds like another word but has a very different meaning

Monologue a long speech in which a character expresses their thoughts. Other characters may be present

Motivation a person's reason for doing something

Objective what a character wants to get or achieve in a scene

Offstage the part of the stage the audience cannot see

Pace the speed at which someone speaks

Paraphrase put a line or section of text into your own words

Pronoun a word (such as *I*, *he*, *she*, *you*, *it*, *we* or *they*) that is used instead of a noun

Pun a play on words

Rhyming couplet two lines of verse where the last words of each line rhyme

Shared lines lines of iambic pentameter shared between characters. This implies a closeness between them in some way

Stage direction an instruction in the text of a play, e.g. indicating which characters enter and exit a scene

Staging the process of selecting, adapting and developing the stage space in which a play will be performed

Statue like a freeze-frame but usually of a single character

Subtext the underlying meaning in the script

Tactics the methods a character uses to get what they want

Themes the main ideas explored in a piece of literature, e.g. the themes of love and friendship, fathers and daughters, justice and mercy, prejudice, deceptive appearances and value might be considered key themes of *The Merchant of Venice*

Tone as in 'tone of voice'; expressing an attitude through how you say something

Vowels the letters a, e, i, o, u